THE E.N.D'S TALE

MICHELLE GODFREY

SPECIAL THANKS

Thank you to my family for pushing me towards my goals. Without your support I would never have made it this far.

CONTENTS

The Eternal Night Dimension known as "The E.N.D", a place hidden far in the Darkest shadows of the Galaxy. A place where the only light is from the thousands of moons and stars above. The purple skies are filled with drifting platform lands created and built by the Royal shadow Kings and Queens of the night.

Shadow born Royals carry the descendent blood of the first Dark Dragon King and the first beautiful Shadow Queen. The story tells that The Dragon King who possesses great powers would morph into a person so that he may walk the lands. His wings were the darkest flame that burn hotter than the stars themselves. He found himself falling in love with a gorgeous woman of the night, The Shadow Queen. She created the worlds and controlled the hottest blazing pink flames. When the King and Queen married and mated, they formed an eternal bond of love. A symbol of bonding appeared on their backs showing proof they are forever in love and bonded for eternity.

The King and Queen, first of the shadows race, gave birth to the new race. They passed down their eternal love and bonding mark to the shadow people of today.

The people of these worlds are born to live by strict rules and laws, separated into different ranks. The common born, nobles, Elders, crimson, healers, and the Royals who are the most important breed.

The Kings and Queens, known as Royals, are born randomly from different families. Their eyes have a special purple glow which shines in the darkness. Royal males are born with dark grey skin and horns of the great Dragon King. They are able to morph into dragons and have the strength of a hundred men. They are the only rulers of the people alongside their Queens. Female Royals are born with astonishing beauty with the longest hair of dark blue. They have darker purple skin than that of common shadow women. Female Royals possess the first Queens powers. They possess the power of creation. Known for their fierce flames and raging tempers, no one will dare fight them.

In today's time, many Royals believe they can marry who they want and live a common life. That has never been the case. Our story begins with a young beauty named Eve, born a Royal, who believes she could run from her fate and change her Destiny. Rebellious of the rules, will she succeed, or fall for her destined love, The Dragon King?

CHAPTER 1

THE HIDDEN ROYAL

The tale begins in a small village hidden within the trees. There lived a man named Charles and his Royal daughter Eve. Charles was a common born man with light grey skin and light blue hair. He wore his long curly hair in a ponytail to the back. His body was strong, and he had a voice of authority. His wife, a Royal born woman, was taken by the Royal guards to marry the Dragon King. Eve and her father tried to live a normal life after that day. The more time passed the weaker Eve's father became. He was aware of the fated bond the Kings and Queens have with each other. Eternal bonds happen instantly with everyone rather they are Common or Royal born. The threads leading to finding your fated love happen often. Sadly, it can never happen with Royals and Commons love. Eve and her father would have nightmares day after day of the night Eve's mother was taken. That very night, Eve would have another.

"No, don't take her! Please, someone stop them! Mom!"

"Eve, wake up!" Charles says.

"Father. I... I was having another nightmare."

Charles sits on the bed and gently caresses his daughter's hair. "Was it about the day your mother was taken?"

"Yes, father. I can't stop thinking about her."

"Eve you shouldn't let that event stop you from living."

"Living? Because of these stupid laws I can never choose my own destiny. Why do I have to be born a Royal? I just want a normal life, not dragged away to marry some king I know nothing about."

"Eve. How long do you really think you can hide your identity?"

"For as long as I live father. I want to have the choice to choose who I love and live where I want."

"Hmm… You do sound like her, your mother. She too hid her identity from the people so that we could live a normal life. But fate didn't care, it wasn't long before she was discovered and taken to marry the Dragon King. Had I not hidden you that day, they would have taken you as well. I don't believe I would have lived this long if they had."

"Father! Don't speak such nonsense."

"My dear daughter, we both know how most die in this world. Should someone murder us, or if your heart is badly broken…that's the end."

Eve walks over to hug her father. She sees the sadness on his face. He tightly hugs her back. "You will always have me by your side father."

"I know my love."

Eve wanted to change the subject to ease the tension.

"Father today is the day the Moon Flowers glow at their brightest. They are so beautiful the way they sparkle in the moon's light and give off the sweetest scent. You know they are my favorite flower on this world. I am going to go pick some in the Illusion Woods. We should go together."

"Eve, wait. We must talk. Please sit down for a moment."

"Well, alright, is something the matter father?"

Eve's father sighs. "I will be leaving today."

"Leave, like to the market or something?"

"No, my dear. I am leaving the village. The only reason I stayed here was to raise and never abandon you as a child. You are a beautiful woman now; I know you will live and find your own happiness."

Eve's tears flow down her cheeks. "Father please don't leave me."

"My child, I shall wipe the tears from your face one final time. You must be strong and know that I love you. I will always love you. Just think of this as my way of finding a new destiny. I will explore and be happy. I can't go on living here without your mother. I leave this home in your possession, take care of it will ya."

"I will take care of this place father, but you must promise me you will live. I won't let you leave unless you promise me."

"I promise, my dear. I love you."

"I love you too father."

That day Eve's father left the village. He would have surely died had he stayed. She knew in her heart that he was barely hanging on to life, for her sake. Now that he is gone, he can start to heal. Eve realizes it was time to start her own journey.

CHAPTER 2

BELOVED FRIENDS

Eve continues her day trying not to morn over her father's departure. She decides it's best to keep living her life as a normal person. That was for the best, she thinks as she strolls through the village market still hiding her identity. Eve wears her normal everyday outfit of a brown hooded cloak that her father made. Underneath she wears her high thigh black shorts, a simple white T-shirt, and brown low heel boots. Her everyday clothes made it easy to blend in with the village people. They were kindhearted people who love Eve. Helping people meant everything to her. The children loved playing catch and tag with her as she was like an older sister to them. This was her home that she wishes to never abandon.

Everyday Eve would hang out with her childhood friends August and Luna. They had been by her side for as long as she could remember. August was an exciting person who sought adventure at every opportunity he could. He always tries his hardest to cheer Eve and Luna up with every chance he has. Though Eve always known August to be hiding something from her and Luna. She would never ask since she too has a secret of her own. August was and average size man with short spiky purple hair. He had light grey skin and with little muscle tone. He had normal purple eyes as do all common shadow people do. She approaches her friend near the entrance of the woods where they hang out.

"Eve over here!" August says.

"On my way August!"

August would often wonder what Eve looked like under her cloak. She was like family to him but never invaded her personal life.

"What does she look like under that cloak." August says in his mind. "I have only seen the bottom of her face for as long as we've been friends. Her voice, so kind and gentle. Often it can come off a little seductive. I don't get the same vibes from her as I do Luna though. Just thinking of how sexy Luna was and her thick hips and thighs make me so hard."

"Hello August."

"Eve! You startled me. How did you get over here so fast?"

"I just ran." Eve says with a slight giggle. "What could you have been thinking about to have you so caught off guard?"

"N- nothing, I wasn't thinking anything at all."

Eve looks at August strangely, she notices the bulge in his pants.

"Oh my! What were you thinking August?" Eve says as she laughs.

"Eve, stop messing around. It was nothing okay."

"Okay, okay, I won't ask again."

He began to blush nervously. He never told anyone how he felt about Luna. He knew he must change the subject.

"Um Eve, could I ask you something?"

"Yeah, of course August? What is it?"

"We have been friends since we were children. Why have you never shown your full face?"

The atmosphere became heavy after August asked the question. Eve thought, why would he suddenly ask such a question. She knew that one day her friends would be curious but today of all days was just bad timing. She was already dealing with her father leaving. He was alone in the world for the first time. She didn't want to answer the question but knew she must give an answer.

"I feel more comfortable covered up August. The other reason is a bit personal."

Eve's voice starts to crack as she speaks.

"Oh no, I can see that I made you uncomfortable. I'm sorry for asking Eve."

"No, don't apologize. I knew someday you would be curious. I am going through some hard times right now."

August and Eve were silent for a moment until they heard a voice in the distance.

"Eve! August!"

"Luna!" Eve and August replies.

Luna was running towards them. She was like a sister to Eve. Eve would come to her for advice. Luna was someone Eve trusted as she always knew how to ease her pain. She is the kindest and strong-hearted person Eve has ever known. Luna was the type of person who would stand up for what she believes in, always willing to help someone in need. The only thing Luna couldn't help, was her weakness for handsome men. She was shorter than Eve with large breasts and wide luscious hips. She had medium purple skin and regular purple eyes. Her hair was light blue and wavy as it flowed down her spine.

Eve smiles. "Luna, I'm so glad you could make it!"

"Oh, come on love, I would never miss hanging out with my two best friends. We always get together every week to pick Moon Flowers, they are your favorite."

"You mean we are your only friends." August says with a grin on his face.

"What did you say!"

August let out a laugh. "I'm just joking Luna, don't hurt me okay."

August and Luna start to wrestle as they tease each other. Eve smiles as she watches her best friends goof around. She let out a small laugh.

"I love being around you two, you mean the world to me, and I love both of you."

"That came out of nowhere. Eve, your tone is different, are you okay?"

"Of course Luna, well…no, I'm not okay."

Eve was always able to talk to her friends about anything. They were someone she could always depend on when she was upset.

"My Father has left the village for good."

"What!" They say shockingly.

"Yes, he wants to explore the different platforms and find happiness."

"Was it because of your mother not being in the village anymore?"

"Yes August. Father's heart was barely hanging on. He couldn't take not having mother by his side. This always happens when a common falls in love with Royals. I hate the laws of our world."

Eve's body becomes tense. Her eyes start to water a bit.

"Eve, I don't intend to offend you, but you know that Royals are destined to be together." Luna explains. "No matter how long or far away they are, they will always be united with their mates. That is just the fate of a Royal born."

"Well, who decides the fate of Royals anyway!"

"Eve never once has raised her voice. This must be a painful subject for her." August says in his mind."

Luna places her hands gently on Eve's cheeks. "Eve, the Royal's fate has always been that way because of the love of the Great Dragon and the Shadow Queen." Luna explains in a gentle tone. "Everyone born is destined to find and love their mate forever. Their passion for one another has spread through the blood of everyone, especially the Royal born Kings and Queens. This is the way things are and it's nobody's fault."

Eve looks at Luna and gives a slight smile. She always had the right words to say.

"Thank you, Luna. You have always known how to make me feel better. I'm sorry for yelling at you."

"Stop. I know you didn't mean it. You are going through a tough time right now. Just know I will always have your back. Everyone in the Village knew you and your father had been hurting for years. We've all admired him for being able to live this long. He hung on for you, Eve. You two would always help the people and kept a smile on your faces even after your mother was taken. The villagers and I love you two and always will."

Eve stares at Luna for a moment. She didn't know the people felt that way about her and her father. Luna's words gave Eve a warm feeling of hope. Her friends were her family, they would stand by her side through these hard times.

"Hey ladies, I hate to interrupt this moment, but we should get going. The night is getting even darker, and we don't want to miss picking the Moon Flowers. You know they only glow at its brightest when the night sky gets even darker."

"Yes, Let's get going." Eve and Luna say.

CHAPTER 3

INTO THE ILLUSION WOODS

The Illusion Woods. A large area of twisted trees with leaves that glowed bright purple and pink. The trees were large enough to fit a small house inside its massive trunk. The Illusion Woods stretch for miles hiding creatures and plants of the unknown. Only the brave would enter a place filled with such beings.

The morning purple sky of night holds the gentle creatures and food for the villagers. But as the sky becomes its darkest night, you will find your life in the hands of the deadliest beast. Each of the floating platforms created by the Royal Queens has their own native creatures. These creatures would mate with other types to form new breeds which everyone has come to fear.

Eve's platform world has their own native creature the shadow wolves known as, "Shadow Walkers". They were known to have killed and eaten hundreds of innocent people. Besides the dangers, these woods were breathtakingly beautiful. Eve and her friends knew if anyone was unfamiliar with these woods would be lost, stuck with the night creatures for days, weeks, or even months. As Eve travels through the woods, she becomes lost in thought. She let out a heavy exhale as she walks.

"The Illusion Woods." She says in her mind. "Luna, August, and I have taken this trip hundreds of times. This place has always amazed me with its beauty. Even if I have done this trip many times alone, it's always best to have someone accompany you just in case you run into trouble. It's not a problem for me since I am a Royal of great power. I can manifest my purple flames through my hand and body as hot as I want. Burning my enemies wouldn't be a problem. Making fireballs is my favorite, I can never find a place to practice using it though."

Eve looks around, she watches out for vicious creatures as she thinks. "If only I could practice in these woods more. Heck even that holds its own dangers. I could accidentally burn the entire woods down. Having to hide who I am and my powers all the time can be exhausting."

Eve looks to the sky, as she sighs. "It's for the best if I want a normal life. I still carry my dual daggers just in case of emergencies. I can fight without harming my friends."

Luna notices Eve's silence as they walk. "Eve, are you alright? It's not like you to be this quiet."

"Yes Luna, I'm fine. I was just lost in thought. I'm fine really, let's continue our journey."

They continue their journey enjoying the scenery until August breaks the silence.

"Hey, do you two remember the first time we entered these woods?"

"Of course." Luna says. "It was all because of that stupid dare you gave to Eve and me. I believe you said we would be too scared to enter these woods, if I am remembering correctly."

"Because of those dumb words we had to prove that we weren't scared." Eve says. "So, like a couple of fools we ran into the woods not knowing what we may have come across."

"Well, it wasn't for nothing." August says. "We were the first to discover all the wonderful plants and creatures the woods had to offer. No other would dare enter this place unless they were the hunters that made the trails. We even discovered Moon Flowers on our world, which so happens to be Eve's favorite flower."

Eve let out a small laugh. "You are right August. We have had some great adventures here. I was overjoyed when we discovered that Moon Flowers grew on our platform. My mother used to love them too. Father would travel to different platforms to get them for her, he didn't even know they grew on our world. Who would have known that they grew next to such a massive lake."

Luna giggles. "Yeah, no one even knew a lake was in these woods until we discovered it. The way it glistens a light blue in the many moons light. I wonder why the lake glows blue, unless it has something to do with the moon flowers or the crystal beneath the surface waters. Either way, it's a magnificent sight to see."

"Maybe we should take a swim when we arrive."

"It seems to me like you are just trying to catch a glimpse of our wet bodies August." Eve says with a slight giggle.

"Well doesn't sound like a bad idea from where I stand."

Luna gives August a hard punch in the arm. "You are such a…"

Luna pauses in her tracks. Before she could finish her sentence, there standing before them was a pack of savage shadow wolves. There were six of them with the seventh being the Alpha. Eve, Luna, and August stared at the Alpha strangely. He didn't look like most Alphas. This one was about 5 feet tall and 4 feet wide. His muscle arms and broad shoulders were of a considerable size. His eyes glowed a blazing fire red with fangs that hung low outside his mouth.

"That Alpha, he must be a hybrid beast." August says.

Hybrid creatures, a mix of the different types of creatures. Some creatures are born from a higher race of the same species. They would mate and give birth to a new race. August, Eve, and Luna all glanced at each other.

August bites down nervously on his bottom lip. "We are so totally screwed."

CHAPTER 4

THE ESCAPE

Eve, Luna, and August stood with their backs against one another. They noticed that the wolves were surrounding them.

Luna began to worry. "What are we going to do? I have always joked about how I would slay any creature that we encounter. Seeing these things up close is terrifying. I have never even killed before; I don't even know how strong these wolves are."

Luna was so frightened; she could barely hold up her dagger. She thought that this was the last time she would see her friends and the people of the village.

"Luna." August says. "I promise I won't let anything happen to you. I have killed a few of these creatures before. This would be my first-time encountering ones this big but it's alright I got you."

Eve was lost in thought while her friends spoke. "Damn. This situation wouldn't be a problem if I could use my flames. If I did that, Luna and August would know who I am. If I don't use my flames, my friends could end up dead. The world just keeps throwing problems my way. Think Eve. If things get worse, I will have no choice but to burn these bastards."

"Eve, look out!" August shouts.

He pushes Eve out of the way and starts to wrestle with one of the wolves. He had his blade between the fangs of the creature to stop it from ripping his head off. August struggles the beast to the ground; he takes out a second blade and stabs the wolf through the heart. It fell dead to the ground after the blow. The Alpha was enraged by the sight and let out an aggressive growl. He howls loudly causing two more wolves to respond by his side.

The two-beast leaps towards Eve and Luna. Eve shoves Luna out the way and dodges the attack. Eve takes out her dual daggers and attacks one of the beasts from behind slicing its head. Luna stands watching August and Eve as they fought, she wanted to join but was terrified. She had practiced using weapons on dummies but never a living creature.

The other shadow wolf turns to attack Luna once more. As it attacks August jumps in front and takes a bite to the arm. He screams in pain but quickly shakes it off. He takes the opportunity to jab his dagger into the throat of the beast.

"Luna, are you ok?"

"Me? What about you? Look at your arm!"

"I will be fine."

"I'm so useless. Because of me you are hurt."

August interrupts her before she could say another word. "Luna, I will protect you no matter what. You don't have to do anything you can't do. I'm here with you."

Luna's eyes began to water. She looks up at Augusts thinking how he was so brave and determined. She had always known him to be a bit of a goof ball, but now, there's an attraction about him that she didn't notice before.

On the other hand, Luna could see Eve was easily fighting off the remaining shadow wolves. At that moment the Alpha stepped forward. He lost over half of his pack. He scowled at Eve ready to attack her. Eve acknowledged that this one was stronger than any other shadow wolves she's fought. She knows she can't fight the Alpha at full strength with her friends around. She came up with a plan to lead it away so she can kill it.

As Eve was thinking of a plan, she heard a scream on the other side. One of the wolves had clawed Lunas's arm. Augusts screamed and jumped on the beast's back. He digs his dagger into its side pulling the flesh away. The Alpha still has his eyes fixated on Eve as she thinks of a plan.

"Here's my chance. I know August will take care of Luna. I must lead this creature away so I can fight."

She takes off running as fast as she can into the woods.

"Eve, no!" August Screams.

Eve runs even faster as the Alpha was hot on her heels. The Alpha was fast and determined to catch its prey.

"One wrong step and I'm done for. I must maintain my distance until I get the chance to strike it."

She continues running through the woods. Looking around she had no idea where she was at this point. All Eve could think about was making sure her friends were safe. Thinking fast, she decided that this was far enough to manifest her flames. She was going to burn this beast to ashes. Before Eve could fully turn around, the Alpha had taken an enormous leap towards her. She gasps as it approaches.

Out from the darkness of the wood, a hooded figure quickly leaps out to tackle the Alpha. The Alpha falls to the ground with great force.

"Impossible!" Eve says in her mind. "No one could be that strong."

Eve looks up at the hooded person from the ground. She could see that this was a man judging from his tall height and broad shoulders. His hood was strangely higher than usual, but Eve didn't worry about that. She wanted to see what would happen next with the Alpha and the strange man.

The Alpha stands face to face with the hooded man, Eve sees the fright in the beast's face. The Alpha tail tucks between its legs as it looks at the man. It was as if he had seen a ghost. It immediately takes off sprinting into the dark woods.

The man turns to Eve an helps her to her feet. "Are you alright?"

His voice was strong with authority, but also gentle. It was a voice that made Eve's heart skip a beat. Eve had never heard a man's voice that made her feel like she was melting.

"Yes, I'm fine, thank you for saving my life."

The hooded man didn't say a word. He stands there staring at Eve.

Eve was confused at why the man was staring at her. "Are you alri..."

Eve pauses. She notices that her hood has fallen back from her face. The man could see Eve's glowing purple eyes and her long dark Royal blue hair. Her lips were full and voluptuous of a light purple. Her eyes were gentle with long thick lashes. She has a cute round face and small button nose. Eve hurries to cover her face.

"Oh No! Please sir don't tell anyone about me!"

"Hmm... Well, this is rather interesting, but your secret is safe with me my lady."

Eve's heart begins to beat harder. "If you don't mind me asking, who are you and what is your name?"

"My name is Max. I traveled here from far away. May I have your name my lady?"

"My name is Eve. I don't live far from here."

"I can't tell him exactly where I live. He may tell someone; I can't take that risk."

"So, um Max, do you know where we are?

Max let out a chuckle. "No, not exactly. I got separated from my party. I too, am lost."

"Well at least we are not alone, right?" Eve says shyly.

"That is true. I'm glad to be stuck here with someone as beautiful as yourself."

Everything about Max made Eve just want to be close to him. His laugh, voice, and strong body was all she could think about. Plus, he was so kind and had a clever way of speaking. She couldn't help but be attracted to him. Eve wonders what face could go with such a hot tone voice. She studies him for a moment, looking at his large muscular arms and tight chest. His hair was dark and around shoulder length. She wanted to know more about him.

"Max? Why do you keep your face covered?"

"I could ask you the same question my lady. Why would a Royal hide her identity? You know, no matter what your mate will always find you."

"There he goes with this "my lady" thing again. Oh, who am I kidding I like that he calls me that. The people of my village only call me Eve, so this is rather refreshing. As for me, I should have known better asking him that question. He was right. I'm asking about his identity and don't really want to share my own. Plus, he doesn't understand that I don't want to be taken to the Palace to marry an unknown King. I want to choose who I love, and no one understands that."

"Sorry I asked such a personal question Max."

"Please, do not apologize. I will answer if you really want to know who I am." Max says in a clever voice.

"No, it's fine."

"No matter who he is or where he's from, he's here now and knows my secret. I can't help but be a little happy that I am around him. I can't put my finger on it, but this man makes me feel so warm inside. Well, I'll think about it later. Until then, we are stuck lost together in the Illusion Woods."

CHAPTER 5

NIGHT IN THE WOODS

They walk for nearly the entire night trying to find their way out of the woods. They had no luck; all they saw was more glowing trees and dense plant life. Max, tired of the silence, decided to start a conversation.

"So, what is a fine lady like yourself doing out here in the woods alone? Of course, knowing you are a Royal, danger must not mean anything to you."

"Well, I didn't come alone. I was with my friends. We were on our way to pick Moon Flowers. That was before we got attacked by the shadow wolves."

"Oh, I am sorry to hear that, will they be alright without you?"

"They will be fine. My friends are stronger than you think."

"You say you were on your way to pick Moon Flowers; they are quite beautiful."

"Yes, they are my favorite flower. My mother use to love them."

"Use to? Is your mother no longer with you?"

"My mother was a Royal as well, she fell in love with my father who is a common. She was discovered and taken to marry the Dragon King. Due to my father living on this world, she decided

29

she didn't want to inherit this platform. Knowing that my father would die from heartbreak in all, she decided to break off and created her own world. Not a day go by that I didn't think of her."

"I am sorry about your mother. Where is your father now; is he not living?"

"My father is alive. He stayed living for my sake. Even though he had to leave our village due to the pain."

"At least you know your parents are still alive." Max says softly.

"Max, what do you mean?"

"My mother and father are no longer in this world. She was a Royal Queen and was assassinated. Soon after my father the Dragon King died from her loss."

Eve clutches her lips with disbelief. She had no idea there are people out there purposely killing others.

"Max, had I known I would have never brought up a conversation about my parents."

Max smiles at Eve. "It is quite alright my lady, it's good that we get to know each other. One day I will find my mother's killer."

Max frowns showing the fangs of his teeth. Just thinking about his mother's killer makes him want to punch something. Eve was still in shock. She heard stories about people killing each other but thought it was just a story to scare the young. Eve thought, how she could be sad when there are people like Max who lost their family. She had more appreciation for her parents still being alive.

"My lady, are you alright, did I say something that offended you?"

"No not at all. I was just thinking about how lucky I am. You are suffering more than I am. I feel so selfish."

"Suffering is suffering no matter how big or small it may be. You have every right to feel just as hurt as I am, my lady."

Max gently grabs her by the chin and smiles. "So don't feel bad."

Eve smiles back at Max. Her eyes lower as she stares at his lips.

"Just who is this man? He seems to have the right words to say. He makes my heart want to sing."

Eve and Max continue their walk under the bright purple moons. They came across a waterfall and some glowing blue berries.

"Look! Glow berries and water!" Eve says with excitement. "I haven't eaten all day, I'm so thirsty too."

Eve kneels and scoops some water into her hands to drink. "The water is so fresh and cold."

Max was staring at Eve with a slight smile. Eve looks over to see him staring at her. Even though she could only see the bottom half of his face, she could tell how incredibly handsome he was. Eve bites her bottom lip as she was thinking and staring at him. She quickly looks away and glances back at the water. Max drinks his portion of water and begins to pick the berries.

"What is wrong with me?" Eve says quietly. "I have been around plenty of men, why is he so different? I can't understand this feeling he's giving."

"My lady, I believe I have gathered enough berries for tonight. We should try and find shelter. The night is only getting darker and colder."

He hands Eve a small brown bag, made of cloth, and full of berries.

"Look over there, there seems to be a small cave." Eve says.

They walk up to the opening of the cave. The back was closed off and was wide enough for the two of them to sleep in.

"We must light a fire, it's getting colder." Max says.

Max gathered some wood and timber for the fire and laid them on the ground in front of the opening. This was so the creatures wouldn't be able to get to them while they sleep. Eve gathers a small pink flame from her hand and lights the fire. Even with the fire, Eve was freezing.

"If it's alright with you my lady, you may snug up next to me."

Eve crawls over to Max and snugs up under his cloak. "Mmm...So warm. I feel better next to you."

"This is rather cozy if I may say."

Max wraps his strong arms around her body. His hands were gentle to the touch as he held her. He starts to rub her body softly. The touch of Max makes Eve's body tremble slightly.

He whispers in her ear. "Is this better my lady?"

Eve can hardly breathe as she replies. "Yes." she whispers. "So much better."

Max holds her more firmly than before. Eve was loving every moment. Every touch he gave her was spectacular. He lowers her hood and begins stroking her long flowing hair. Her eyes roll as he caresses her.

"He's doing this on purpose. His touch is driving me crazy."

Eve caresses Max's hand as he holds her. He delicately pulled her back by the hair. He stares at her as she looks towards him. He leans down and kisses her soft lips. Eve let out a small moan.

"His kiss is so soft and gentle."

They continue to kiss as their tongues dance around with one another. Max pulls away slowly, still leaving his lips close to hers.

"Wah, what is this feeling you're giving me? I just met you, yet this feels so right, so good."

"Maybe there's a reason for that my lady."

Max turns Eve around and mounts her on top of him. "I must have her." He says in his mind. "Her soft body and lips feel amazing. I don't think I can hold back my feelings for her."

Eve grabs Max's face and kisses him more intensively. He grabs her hips and moves her body to grind on his penis. Eve can feel Max's hardness from his pants. She continues to grind on him as he sucks and licks up and down her neck. Max lifts Eve's shirt and begins to rub her large breast.

Eve has never felt pleasure such as this before. She didn't want it to end. Her hands strolled down his muscled tight chest down to his hard penis. Eve could feel how big he was. Max lets out a moan as she rubs his hardness. Eve took pleasure in hearing Max's moan. Max lay Eve on her back and continues licking and sucking her body. He bites the bottom of her lip then forces his tongue into her mouth.

"No. I must control myself. I can't allow this to be our first time. I must be patient. Even though she feels so damn good."

Max suddenly stops and stares down at Eve breathing heavily.

"What's wrong?" Eve says with curiosity.

"We can't let ourselves get carried away. I don't want our first time to be in some old cave lost in the woods."

Eve pouts at the situation. Max chuckles at her pouty face. Eve didn't want to stop, but she knows in her heart Max was right.

"Let us sleep my lady, we can save that energy for the morning."

"Yeah, I guess you're right."

They snuggle up together and fall fast asleep.

The next morning Max wakes before Eve. He stares at her beauty once more. "I've finally found you...my Queen."

Max moves the hair from her face and kisses her forehead. he whispers. "Till we meet again, my lady."

Max hurries as he hears the voices calling for Eve.

"Eve! Eve!"

Eve wakes to hear August and Luna calling for her. "August! Luna! Max, wake up, those are my..."

Before Eve could finish, she looks over to see Max was gone. In his place laid a note.

"Why is this here? Let's see what it says."

My Lady,

"I'm sorry to leave so suddenly. I could hear your friends calling for you. I'm sure you will be safe with them. I must get back to my party, they are waiting for my return. I promise I will see you again. We are destined for each other, and I know you felt the same. See you soon, my love."

Sincerely, Max

"Well, this is surprising. I hope I do see him again."

CHAPTER 6

BACK TO THE VILLAGE

"Eve!" August and Luna say with concern.

"August, Luna, what a relief. Your both are alright."

Eve embraces her friends. They all hold each other for a moment. Eve can see the exhaustion on their faces. They were searching for her all night.

"What were you two thinking? You could have been lost in these woods for months looking for me. Plus, both of you are badly injured."

"There was no way we were going back to the village without you Eve." August says. "Luna and I left a trail so that we may find our way back home."

"Eve, you must have been freezing out here." Luna says. "Not only was you alone in the dark, but you also had that Alpha chasing you. What happen to the Alpha anyway?"

"It lost my trail when I was running."

Eve didn't want to mention that she was not alone in the woods. She had Max with her. All she could think about was if he was safe and when she could see him again.

"What was you thinking running off like that? You could have been killed by that creature."

"I am fine August. I would rather it had been me killed then the two of you."

"Don't speak like that!" Luna says. "We could have fought the Alpha together than have you die by that beast. You are not alone, remember."

Eve smiles, her friends were so loyal to her. They would do anything for her. She wondered if she could let them know her secret. In her heart she knew they wouldn't say a word.

"Um, we should get going ladies. The Alpha is still running free out here and I am starting to grow tired of this place."

Both Eve and Luna agree. They made their way out of the cave. Eve looks down and notices there was a single Moon Flower left at the side of the entrance.

"Max." she says softly.

***

A few days later, in the Palace of the lands, Max sat on the throne. "Have you found her yet?"

"No, my king, we checked out two of the three villages of the area." The guardsmen say. "She wasn't there, so we burned and slayed the people."

"She must be in the last village. I will accompany you on this trip. I must see her."

A week passed and Eve was still wondering if she would ever see Max again. She remembers his touch and his gentle kiss. She could still remember the way he handled her body as if he already owned her. Her heart was crying with pain from not being next to him. Eve sat at the dinner table where she and her father would share a meal and conversate. It felt strange knowing he wasn't there anymore. Suddenly, there was a knock at the front door.

"Eve, are you home?"

"Yes, be there in a moment Luna."

Eve reaches for her brown cloak to cover her face. She opens the door to see Luna and August standing there with some food.

"Wow! You two are looking much better. Your wounds, they look almost fully healed."

"Yeah, the doctor said our arms will fully heal in no time." Luna says.

"I kind of like my scar. It makes me look like a badass."

Luna rolls her eyes at August comment. "Sure, of course, it does."

They all let out a laugh.

"Eve, we haven't heard from you in a week." Luna says. "We were worried about you, so we brought you some food and a little gift."

"Mmm… Is that berry pound cake and meat stew I smell? Well, you two are being generous today, come right on in."

"Here Eve, this is for you. It's a bracelet I made myself from blue crystals. I know you've been feeling down so I thought this might cheer you up."

"Thank you, Luna! I will treasure this always."

They sat around the table enjoying what Eve would consider, the best pound cake she's ever had." They were eating a beef stew with vegetables in a thick gravy sauce. Suddenly they heard a commotion outside the door. The people were screaming in panic. Eve, Luna, and August rush to the window.

Eve's eyes widen. "Oh No! I remember that Armor well. It's the Royal Guards!"

CHAPTER 7

THE ROYAL GUARDS

A guardsman stands at the top of a wooden stage and shouts to the villagers. "People of the village! We are here to retrieve the next Royal Queen! We have word that she is of age for marriage and may be living in this very village!"

The townspeople whisper to each other with confusion. They began to panic. They are aware of the laws and rules of the worlds. If the Queen is not of their village, their homes and the people will be killed.

There are rules and laws people must follow about Royals and villages. Once a Royal is born, the Palace is notified. The village in which the Royal was born is taken care of by the new King and his Queen. If they do not wish to inherit the platform of their birth, then they will have the choice to leave. The Queen and King will take the people who want to leave and break off to create a new floating platform. The lands they see floating in the distant sky is because of this decision. The only downfall to the rules is villages in different areas of the land must perish. They are known as bad blood because no Royal was born from the people. If they are lucky, they would hear about where a Royal was born and move to that village before they are discovered. That is, if they are lucky. Those have always been the rules.

The guard spoke once more. "May the new Queen step forward. You must be taken to the Dragon King for marriage."

A villager steps forward to speak. "Please sir, we have no knowledge of a Royal being born here yet."

"Then you shall all perish!"

The guard gestures his hands for the soldiers to burn their homes and kill the villagers. They ready their swords and flame arrows. The men took aim at the people's homes. They fired a shot and set flames to one of the homes. The people scream and panic with fear. Eve watches, as the guards terrorize her home. She couldn't believe this was happening. The people were always so kind and cared for her and her father. They were like family. She couldn't let them pay for her mistake. Before Eve could think she shouts out at the guards.

"Stop! For I am the Queen you seek!"

Eve pulls off her hood and reveals herself to the guards. She shows her glowing purple eyes and long dark Royal blue hair that fell to her lower thighs. She has a perfect hourglass figure with thick thighs and perfect round ass. Eve's breast was a D cup and set up perfectly on her chest.

The townspeople were astonished by her beauty. They were in disbelief that Eve was the Queen this whole time. The villagers began to kneel and bow their heads. Eve looks at all of them until she lays eyes on her best friends.

"August, Luna, I'm so sorry I hid this secret from you. I didn't want you to be involved with me hiding my identity. I know you two would have kept my secret safe. I just wanted to live a normal life and stay here with you two and the villagers. And for as all my village friends, I am sorry I put you through this."

"It would be our honor to have you as our Queen!" A man shouts.

"Yeah, we love you, Eve!" The villagers shout.

Eve almost fell into tears by the support of the people. "I wish I could stay. I've hid long enough."

August steps in front of Eve holding his hand to block the guards. "Then you shouldn't leave."

"August! What are you doing?"

"You shouldn't be forced to leave and marry anyone you don't want to."

Walking up to August was a tall muscular man. The atmosphere changes when he walks. His eyes were fierce, and his jawline was strong and firm. There was a scar on his left cheek and a frown upon his face. His hair was low on the sides with short length curly hair on the top of his head. The curls from his hair covered the front side of his forehead. Eve thought he would be quite handsome if he wasn't scowling at his friend with intention to kill.

"You best step away from the Queen boy." he says in a deep stern voice.

August legs start to tremble from the fearsome aura the guard was giving off. His voice was heavy with authority. It was a voice that would strike fear in his enemies.

"Did you not hear me boy? I said step away from the Queen!"

The guard's voice growled with aggression when he spoke to August.

"August." Eve says softly. "Step away now. This guard is serious, and I don't want you hurt."

August looks back at Eve, shocked by her words. He saw that she was worried for his safety. He understands her feelings and steps away.

The guard was still holding the hilt of his sword staring at August. He fixes his eyes on Eve, steps forward and kneels.

"My apologies my Queen. My name is Garret. I am the head guardsman and right-hand man of the Dragon King. I was sent to bring you back to the Palace to be wedded to my King."

As Garret spoke, Eve was thinking.

"How could this be happening." she states in her mind. "I was so careful in hiding my identity. The only one who saw me was Max. No, it couldn't be. I trusted him. He wouldn't do this right? Was Max a spy for the Dragon King all along? I thought…he loved me. How could I have been so stupid."

"My Queen, we should get going."

"Before I go anywhere with you!" Eve says aggressively. "Will my village be safe!?"

"Yes, my Queen, that is the way. The Royal's home is to not be touched. This was your home, correct?"

"Yes, it was." Eve says softly.

"Before I go, I must retrieve some things of importance from my home."

"Very well. I will accompany you. I wouldn't be surprised if you tried to run. If that was to happen, I will have no choice but to order this village to be burn and the people killed."

"What an asshole." Eve thought.

"I'm not going to run; you can come if you wish."

Eve enters her home and packs a few of her belongings. She went into her father's room to retrieve a small wooden box which held his pocket watch. She opened the drawer and picked up a velvet box that held her mother's pearl necklace. She made sure to grab the bracelet that Luna had made for her. She makes her way back to Garret and looks him straight in the face.

"I'm ready. Now, let's go meet this king of yours."

CHAPTER 8

THE ROYAL PALACE

Eve says her goodbyes to the villagers and her friends. She holds Luna and August tightly and wishes them well. Tears fall from their faces.

Eve forces a smile on her face. "I will write to you two, so make sure you write me back."

"This isn't fair. You shouldn't be forced to this."

"It's ok August. At least I know my home will be safe. All of you are my family, and I will do anything to protect you and my home."

August and Luna watch as Eve walks away. Eve walks over to the carriage and steps inside. She looks across to see a handsome man smiling at her. He had long slightly curved horns coming from his head. His skin was dark grey, and his eyes were kind and glowed a bright purple. He had shoulder-length dark grey hair. His fangs were sharp, and his jawline was strong.

"The Dragon King." Eve said softly.

"Oh, do you not recognize me...my lady."

"Max!" Eve says surprisingly.

Eve was lost for words. She recognizes that low gentle tone anywhere. Of course, he always calls her, My Lady. There in front of her was the man she thought about for days. She would flash back to the very night she met him. She knew he was handsome but after seeing him like this she couldn't help but want him more. Her heart begins to race nervously with excitement.

"My lady, would you care to sit next to me. It's been a week since I have last touched you and smelled your scent."

Eve's nerves were getting to her. She moves over to sit next to him. He was well dressed in a black button-up shirt with golden trims around the edges. Over his shirt was a black vest with golden crimson flowered patterns down the sides. His shoes had a shine that was enough to reflect the surface of the world.

Eve was feeling out of place sitting next to him. All she had was a short black shirt and a brown skirt with brown boots for travelling in the woods. Covering all of that was her brown cloak.

Max was eager to get his hands on her. He didn't care what she was wearing. He kissed and caresses all over her body. He leans in towards her neck, smelling and licking her. Eve couldn't get a word in as Max started to devour her lips. Eve let out a moan as their tongues play with one another. Max gave her legs a squeeze as he continued to caress her. He pulls away from her slowly and looks into her gentle eyes.

"I've missed you, my lady. Being away from you was driving me mad. I've waited long enough to feel your lips and soft skin again. This time I won't be holding back on you. Then again, maybe I'm coming on to strong."

Max chuckles and smiles at Eve.

"No." Eve says softly. "I have wanted to feel this as well. I thought I would never see you again. Heck, I thought you were a spy for the king. Now I see you was the King this whole time."

"Well, I did offer to tell you. You told me never mind, remember?"

Eve gives Max a little shove and laughs. "You are such a jerk." she says jokingly.

Max and Eve laugh as they enjoy each other's company.

"My Queen, please allow me to officially introduce myself. My name is Maximillian Dracon the 3rd."

Eve was impressed with such a name. She thought soon she would be taking on his name very soon.

"So, shall I call you Maximillian or Max?"

"You can call me whatever you please, my lady."

"Well, my name is Eve Divine. Eve says shyly. I know it's not as impressive as yours."

"No... Your name suits you well. You are quite a divine woman."

Eve blushed a little. She thought that was such a cheesy line, yet somehow, he made it work. She couldn't help but giggle.

"Was that line a bit much?" he says with a smile.

"Maybe a little."

Max continues admiring Eve's beauty. They enjoy each other until they finally reach the Palace.

"My King we are arriving at the Palace." A guardsman says.

Eve felt sick to her stomach. She was more nervous than before. She acknowledges this was now her new home. What if she doesn't like it here or the people were cruel. The carriage stops, a servant opens the door for them. Eve steps out to see an enormous well-lit Palace in front of her. Her mouth drops at the beautiful view of the gardens and fountains. The Palace was a sparkling blue with Moon Flowers on the sides of the entrance. There in the middle of the courtyard lays a massive fountain. It had a dragon in the middle shooting water from its mouth.

All the Royal guards stood in line side by side with their fists to their chests. All the Palace servants stood on the stairs of the entrance. They bow their heads as we approach. Eve was still nervous as she and Max walked pass the servants.

"Welcome home your Royal greatness." The servants say all at once.

Eve was speechless. She wonders why there wasn't a woman in sight. Then Eve remembered that wasn't allowed. Royal Queens can be very jealous. If she suspects another female around their King, it would literally be the end of the world. The Queen has the power to break and destroy the world. You wouldn't want to anger them.

Max escorts Eve into the Palace. "My lady. Let me introduce you to your personal servants."

Eve was still surprised that they were all male. She looks at Max with concern. Max sees the worry on her face.

"Do not worry my lady. These men are different. I would never allow anyone other than them to care for you. I would never put you in harm's way. Let me introduce your personal maid. He is the head of all the servants and maids."

"Ronzell!"

Ronzell springs out of the crowd with loads of energy. "Heyyy. It is so nice you meet you your highness."

"Wait. You are."

"Beautiful! Yes, I know, I was born that way." Ronzell says interrupting Eve.

Eve realizes that her maids were what was known as, "Queens men". They are very kind people with great strength and determination. They have amazing cooking skills, fashion sense, and are well trained in combat. Eve's mom had told her about men like them, but she had never met one until now. As she observes Ronzell, she notices his sassy way of talking and full of confidence. He was beautiful and tall. He had shoulder length light blue hair with bangs that covered one eye. His nails were an inch long like claws of a shadow cat.

Ronzell was eager to serve Eve. "Oh, no, no, no. What are you wearing my Queeny?"

"Um, clothes."

"Queeny you are a Royal. We are going to get you into something more suited for a beautiful woman like yourself. I refuse to have my Queen looking like she's going on a hike in the woods or something."

"My King do you mind if I get the Queen dress in something less, well, rags and bags."

"Hey." Eve says putting her hands on her hips.

Max let out a laugh. "Of course, Ronzell. Give her something more appropriate for dinner tonight. I wish to spend the evening with my future wife."

"Just leave her to me your majesty."

CHAPTER 9

A PLACE FOR EVE

Ronzell escorts Eve to her room. Eve stops to admire her room. She thought about how huge it was. There was a wide framed door that led to an outside balcony. The closet was large enough to fit several other people's belongings inside. The bathroom had white marble flooring and its own private jacuzzi with feline fountain statues for the water flow. There was a shower area that looked like a waterfall flowing from the ceiling.

The next room connected to the bathroom was the hot spring. It was made from dark wood trees and a dark stone pathway leading to the bath. Eve walks to where her bed was, it was large enough to fit at least ten people.

"Wow, this is all mines Ronzell? How could you fit all of this in one room? This room is bigger than my home back in the village."

"Well, this is just one room. There are over a hundred more."

"A hundred!"

"Yes. Now Queeny if you don't mind stepping out of those raggedly clothes."

"Sure, but please take care of my cloak. It was made by my father and means a great deal to me."

"As you wish love." Ronzell claps his hands twice.

Two maids enter the room and slightly bows their heads. "You call Madam?"

"Yes. Take these rags, I mean the Queens clothing and have them clean. Bring them back once you're finished."

Eve steps into the shower to clean before her bath. She enjoys the way the water falls onto her body like the rain from the sky. She takes a moment to relax and think. When Eve was finished, she went to sit in the warmth of the bath. Eve moans with satisfaction. She exhales when she lays back into the hot water that massages her body.

"This feels amazing. I really needed this relaxation after all the stress I've been enduring."

"Well, you should get used to this feeling. All of this is yours, so enjoy it."

"Ronzell, how long have you been a maid?"

"Oh, girl for as long as I can remember. I've been serving the King for as long as he was searching to find you my dear. Between you and me, he would also go out searching for some bad guy."

"Bad guy?"

"Who could this bad person be?" Eve says in her mind.

"Is Max in some sort of danger?"

"Well, don't you go worrying your beautiful little head over it. You must be ready for your romantic dinner with your King tonight."

Eve smiles at the thought of spending an evening with Max. She couldn't wait to see his smile and hear his charming voice.

"What should I wear?"

"You just leave that to me. I'm about to make you irresistible to the King."

Ronzell snaps his fingers twice to call for the maids to enter. "I need y'all to bring me my hair supplies, nail polish, and a robe for the Queen. Hurry, hurry, now."

They brush Eve's hair while massaging her feet and painting her nails. The maids gave Eve the spa treatment that women would beg for. They were gossiping and laughing as they talked about the Palace living. Eve didn't feel uncomfortable as she thought she would be. They were like friends she enjoys being around.

When all was done, they begin dressing Eve in a sexy black slick dress. It hugs all her curves with the back of the dress expose. There was a leg split on the right side with pink flower petals designed on that area. They button the strap around her neck that holds her dress up. Her hair was fixed in a wrapped-up bun with bangs hanging on the sides of her face. There was a pink flowered ribbon wrapped around her bun.

"You, look, stunning my Queen." Ronzell says holding his hand to his lips.

The other maids clap with approval.

"Are you ready for your date Queeny?"

"Yes, I'm ready. I know this is going to be a night I will remember. I can't wait to see Max."

CHAPTER 10

DINNER FOR TWO

Eve's maids escort her outside of the Palace. There, waiting far in the distance, was Max with a bouquet of flowers. Max was wearing an oxford blue shirt and a smokey grey vest. His pants were dark oxford blue to match his top. His shoes were black with a smokey grey pattern. Max was standing next to a table decorated with candles and red rose petals. The night was clear with every star and moon visible. Eve couldn't think of a more romantic scenery.

"Talk about a first date." Eve mumbles softly as she walks. "I would have never imagined any of this ever happening. Me, living in the Palace, madly in love with the King. I spent my life avoiding ever meeting the King. Now look at me, He takes my breath away when I'm around him. I hate being far from him."

Eve finally approaches Max and admires how amazing he looks. He didn't say a word at first. He was busy looking her up and down craving her body.

Max was lost in thought. "Wow! She looks even more desirable than before. I didn't even realize the curves on her body. Her breast, so round and perfect. My gosh, look at those thighs. Her hair, her beauty, she's breathtaking. I can't wait to have her as my wife."

"Hello Max." she says shyly.

"Hello my lady. You look astonishing tonight."

Eve blushes from his words. He lifts her hand and plants a gentle kiss upon it. Still holding her hand, he leads her to her seat and pulls out her chair. Max walks to his seat and sits across from her. He looks across the table to see Eve's eyes reflecting the moons within them. Max wanted her so badly he could hardly stand it.

Eve could see the expressions on Max's face as he bit his bottom lip. She felt a little exposed having that she hid under a cloak growing up. This was a new feeling for her. She finally feels free and true to herself. This was who she was. Her mind and body were relaxed around Max and the people of the Palace.

Max didn't want to make Eve any more nervous than she already was. Her body language was telling him everything. He starts a conversation to break the ice. "I'm certainly lucky to have found such a beautiful future wife. Why don't we continue to get to know each other."

"What more would you like to know?"

"Everything."

Before Eve could speak, the servants were ready to serve them their food. Infront of Eve was a plate with a perfectly glaze steak with herbs and vegetables on the sides.

Eve looked like a predator as she studies her food. Max let out a chuckle.

"Maybe we should enjoy our meal first, then talk."

Eve shakes her head in agreement. Eve slices into the tender juicy meat. She takes her first bite of the tender meat and pauses. She closes her eyes as she savors the moment of the first bite. She couldn't believe the amount of flavor bursting from the meat. Moments after, she takes a bite to taste the veggies. The flavors were well balanced to complement the steak.

"This is so delicious! Please tell the chef this is the best food I have ever had!"

"Well thank you my lady."

"Wait? Why are you saying thank you?"

"Well, I am the one who prepared this meal. I learned from my mother."

Eve thought to herself for a moment. "So, he's good looking, can cook, great kisser, there is no way he could be so perfect. There must be more to him, right? Either way I feel as if I could marry him right now. This food is something I would purposely have him cook for me."

"Is there something on your mind my love?"

"No, it's nothing."

Eve couldn't wait any longer, she wanted to try the dessert. The servants placed a plate of dessert in front of her with a glass of Sparkle Berry wine next to it. Eve was always fond of sweet food. She observes the cake presented to her for a moment. It was a chocolate glazed cake with purple glow berries and a glow leaf on top. They were the rarest type of berries to be found on their world. She takes her knife and slices down the moist cake. Taking the first bite of the cake almost made Eve shed a tear. The sweetness gave Eve a favorable feeling. The wine balances the sweetness of the cake making them the perfect combination.

"I could have this meal forever!"

Max laughs at her excitement. "I'm glad you enjoy my cooking. There will be much more where that came from."

Eve squints her eyes at Max. "Let's not get cocky okay." she says as she turns her nose to the sky.

Max found her humor attractive. He couldn't help but smile as he enjoyed her company. "Eve my love, let's continue where we left off. Tell me more about you."

"Well, you already know about my parents and that I hid my identity."

"Why were you hiding again?"

"Because of what happened to my mother. After she was forcefully taken from my father, I decided I wanted to choose my own future. I didn't want to marry someone I didn't know. I also didn't want my father to die or be alone. I just wanted to live a normal life with him."

Eve looks away from Max as she tries not to tear up. "My father used to make my clothes and wipe my tears when I was sad about my mother. Many nights he stayed up comforting me as I missed her. I knew He loved me unconditionally. Soon after my mother was taken, all I had was my father and my two best friends August and Luna.

My friends and I grew up together like family. We would discover the wonders of the world. My village was kind, and no one ever questioned why I hid my face. I will surely miss everyone."

Max stares at Eve, feeling her pain. "Do you regret your decisions, or being here with me?"

"No! I love being here with you. But I don't regret hiding either. I met so many great people, and I wouldn't be who I am today if it wasn't for my decision. I wouldn't have met and fell in love with you if I was discovered."

"You, Love me?"

Eve didn't even realize she had admitted her true feelings for Max. She pauses before she answered.

"Yes, I do." she says softly.

Max rises to his feet and walks over to Eve. He slightly raises her chin and kisses her lips gently.

"I was hoping you felt the same way for me as I do for you. I love you as well, my lady. I will do whatever I can to be the greatest husband for you."

Eve was speechless. She stares into his eyes; she was lucky to have fallen in love with Max before she was taken. Otherwise, her story would have been different. Her heart was pounding faster than she could count. His words had filled her with a warm feeling of happiness.

"So Max, what about you? What's your life's story?"

Max walks back to his seat. "Well, it is how you see it today, I was born and raised in the Palace. My mother and father where both Royals. They spoiled me rotten, giving me whatever I ask for. I never took it for granted, I appreciated everything I received. My mother would sing to me in the loveliest voice. She showed me how to cook and garden. My father taught me to fight and morph into my dragon form. He taught me to be humble and kind so that I may make a great King someday. I would often run away and explore the lands, that of course worried my mother."

Max chuckles thinking of his younger self. He then takes on a more sadden look. "That life quickly came to an end. I was out training with my now, head of the guards Garret, when we heard my father's roar. Garret and I ran into the Palace towards my parents' room. My father was fighting a man with a white cloth on his face. He clawed at the man's chest leaving a deep wound. My father pulled the cloth from his face revealing his identity. I caught a glimpse of his face before he jumped out the window. My father morphed into his dragon form and flew after him. I wondered what that man could had done to anger my father. I looked over at the floor to see my mother was dead. That man had assassinated my mother."

Max balls up his fist as he thinks of that moment. "As you know yourself Eve, there are common shadows that fall in love with the Royals. You know that when Royals find their other mate they bond for life and destine to be together. There are common born who believe that's not fair to them. There was a woman who loved my father and was jealous when my father found and married my mother. My father's men believed she may have been the one who hired an assassin to kill my mother. It wasn't like my father was in love with her. That woman fell in love with his looks when she saw him talking to the villagers one day. Her love was nothing but fake feelings. It was all for nothing, that woman found another to bond with who suddenly died. She eventually died from heartbreak so I never could get my revenge."

"With the Queen dead our land that my mother built and created on began to crumble and fall apart. My father flew to the Palace and took me and as many people as he could hold on to his back. Ever other person living on the platform died that day."

"My father flew to the platform we are on today since there was no Queen or King on it. This land was left behind by a past Queen. My father held me close to his heart with tears in his eyes. He told me he loved me, but he would soon die without my mother. He left me in Garret's care as he flew off into the darkness of space. We began to build the Palace you see before you and started a new life. I swore that day that I would find my mother's killer."

Max looks over to Eve. His eyes widen as he sees the tears falling from her face. He rushes over to her and holds her tight.

"Eve! Are you alright? I am so sorry. This was supposed to be and happy occasion. I shouldn't have told you everything so soon."

Eve stands and kiss Max firmly on the lips. "I'm happy you were comfortable enough to share your story with me Max. I didn't know how much you've suffered. I promise I will always be here for you. I will stand by your side through all the hard times."

Max holds her tight in his arms. "Those are welcoming words to hear my love. I can't wait to marry you."

"Me too. So, when are we to be married?"

"Well, tomorrow of course." he says with a smile.

"Wait! What!"

CHAPTER 11

EVE'S REALIZATION

Eve paces the floor nervously back and forth.

"Um, Queeny, don't you think you've paced the floor long enough." Ronzell says. "You keep this up you're going to walk a hole in the floor."

"Everything is moving so fast. First my father leaves, I get attacked by wolves, taken from my home, and now, I have a wedding tomorrow. I feel like someone is just toying with my life."

"Well, that's the life of a Royal born honey."

Ronzell walks over to Eve and places his hand on her shoulders. "I need you to calm down and breathe."

They both inhale and exhale together.

"Now listen, you need to stop being so hard on yourself. You are the kindest woman I've ever known. You tried to run from your fate and failed. Let it go. You should be thinking about the future and make the best of your new life. I can see you're going to be an amazing Queen. So, own your life."

Eve took a deep breath as she understood Ronzell's words. Eve Respected him and how he cares for her feelings. Eve thought she should try and do everything in her power to be the best Queen for her people. Finding someone she truly wants to marry was lucky enough. The only thing left was to do her part as a Queen.

"Ronzell, thank you. I have been under so much stress lately. I haven't had a chance to really think. There are so many rules and laws to being a Royal that it's hard to keep up with them all. It's not like there is a book out there with all the rules in them."

"Well...actually."

"Ronzell! Not another word."

Ronzell and Eve shared a laugh and a hug. Moments later there was a knock at the door.

"Come in." Ronzell says.

"Madam, it's time for us to get the Queens measurements for her gown. We must hurry if we are to finish in time." The maid says.

"Ohhh, yes, yes, yes! It's time to get started. This is the exciting part. Queeny I'm about to make you the most outstanding dress for tomorrow."

"How will you finish by tomorrow?"

"Just leave all of it to me and my crew."

Ronzell claps his hands twice for the maids to get everything ready. They begin taking Eve's measurements and talking about colors and designs.

"All finish. We have so much to do Queeny, so try and get some rest. See you in the morning."

"Thank you, Ronzell. See you then."

Eve exhales and sits on the bed. She finally got a chance to be alone and was exhausted from everything that had happened. Just before she could lay down and rest a guardsman enters the room.

"Um, is there something wrong?"

"Not at all my Queen." The guard says licking his lips. "I am here for you my dear. You are more beautiful than I imagined."

"What are you doing? Come no closer or I will burn your face off you creep!"

"You will do nothing of the sort! It's not fair that your kind gets to wed the King and not a common like myself. I will take what I want in this world."

He rushes over and grab Eve's wrist. He wrestles her to the floor trying to rip away her clothes. Eve manifests her flames and burns the man's face. The man screams in agony.

"Ahh, you bitch! I'm really going to have my way with you now!"

Suddenly out from the shadows a rope was wrapped around the guard's throat. It was Ronzell with a determine look on his face. He tightens the rope with great strength until Eve hears a snap. The guard falls dead to the floor.

"Ronzell!" Eve says with relief.

She rushes over to him and squeezes him tightly. Ronzell holds Eve and rubs her hair.

"It's okay love, nobody is going to mess with my Queen."

CHAPTER 12

PREPARATIONS

Max was informed of what had occurred in Eve's room. He rushes to her room and embraces her.

"Eve!" He squeezes her tightly in his arms. "Eve, I'm terribly sorry for what has happened tonight. I promise this will never happen again."

Eve looks up to see Max's frowning face. She could see the rage and anger upon it. His eyes were glowing brighter than ever before, and his claws were extended. Eve was almost frightened by the fierceness of his presence. She touches Max's face gently and looks into his eyes. She didn't want him to worry about her.

"I'm fine my love." Eve says in a gentle tone. "I had Ronzell here to protect me. He's an amazing maid and a loyal friend."

Max looks over to Ronzell and gives a nod of approval. Ronzell bows his head slightly and curtsy. Max takes Eve's hand and kisses it.

"I promise I will never let harm come to you again. I will have Ronzell and the maids keep an eye on your room while I evaluate the castle. For now, get some rest, we do have a wedding to attend."

Max smiles at Eve. She could see he was trying to hide the fact that he was still furious. He wanted Eve to rest and know that she would be safe living in the Palace with him. Tomorrow was a special day. He wasn't going to let anyone ruin it for them.

Max kisses Eve passionately before him and Garret takes their leave. He gently shuts the door and frowns angrily.

"Garret."

"Yes, my King."

"Walk with me."

"As you wish, my King."

Max walks the Palace halls with Garret speaking of what actions to take next.

"Are you familiar with the guard who attacked my Queen?"

"Yes, I do know of him and his family."

"Good." Max says with a fearsome tone. "See to it that his friends, family, and whoever is associated with him are all slaughtered tonight. Slaughter any guards you suspect of betraying the Palace. Kill any guards who are friends with him. Inform everyone that this is the punishment for anyone who attacks me and my family."

"Yes, my King, I shall see to it tonight."

CHAPTER 13

THE MORNING OF THE WEDDING

The next morning Eve wakes to the sight of the bright moons. Her bed was so soft as if she was sleeping on a cloud. Ronzell burst through the room cutting on all the lights. Eve shields her face from the sudden brightness.

"Today, is the day! We have so much work to do! We must get you cleaned, do your hair and nails, ah, busy, busy, busy!"

Ronzell rushes Eve to the bathing room to clean her. The maids where trimming and painting her nails, while Ronzell was how he would say, "Works his magic", on Eve's hair. When they were finished it was time for Eve to fit into her gown. She turns and faces the body mirror. She gasps at the sight of herself. She didn't know she could look so beautiful.

Eve's gown accentuates every curve of her body. She wore and off the shoulder lace, heart shaped top, with a slim corset fit waist that led into a ball gown bottom. Her white dress was covered with light blue sparkling diamonds that shimmered in the moon's light. Her train and veil flow long across the floor with the moon flower design on it. The maids place her blue diamond crown upon her head to top it off.

"Ronzell." Eve says faintly. "This dress is beyond my expectations. I don't know if I could thank you enough."

"It was my pleasure darling."

Ronzell was fanning his eyes trying not to tear up. He finally created a dress worthy of a Queen. He was proud that Eve could wear it. The maids all claps with appreciation of Ronzell's work.

"May I have a moment to myself?"

"Of course, you may Queeny." Ronzell snaps his fingers for all the maids to leave the room.

Eve took a moment to admire herself. "Something's missing."

She went over to the drawer to grab her mother's pearl necklace and put it on. "There, perfect, now I have a piece of you with me mother."

Eve realizes her life is about to change. She was missing her father, thinking he would love to watch this big moment in her life. Her father would have laughed at her. She hid for so long and now; she would be Queen of the lands. As Eve was thinking to herself, there was a knock at the door. A guardsman slowly opens the door.

Eve looks back at the door. "Come in."

"Your highness, one of the Royal Queens wish to speak with you."

"Um, sure, show them in please."

Eve was confused. "What Queen would want to see me?"

The Queen walks through the door and smiles. "It's so good to see you again my dear."

Eve's eyes widen. "Mother!"

CHAPTER 14

EVE'S PERFECT WEDDING

"How, when did you get here mother? How did you know it was my wedding?"

"Eve." her mother says with a gentle soft tone. "Your King sent an invitation to all the neighboring platforms. When I saw your name, I knew I had to attend. I had to see you again and hope you are not angry with me."

"No! I would never be angry with you. I know now that you have a bond with your king. I feel the same about Max. You had to leave me and father."

"How is Charles?"

"Father is fine. He left the village and now travels alone."

Eve's mother put her hand to her heart. "Thank goodness. He lives. Oh, are those my pearls, goodness I haven't seen them in years. They fit you well my dear. I'm glad you could wear them on this special day. Maybe you can pass them on to your daughter someday."

Eve smiles at her mother. "Thank you, mother. But where have you been living this whole time?"

"I live on the northern sky island next to this one. There was no way I could be any farther from you. Not a day went by that I didn't miss and think of you."

Eve's mother had tears rolling down her face. Eve walks over and hugs her. She still had the warmth and love Eve remembers as a child. Eve hadn't forgotten her mother's sweet scent of fresh flowers. She felt comfortable like a child again in her mother's arms.

"Mother, just seeing you here is comforting. I was so nervous and alone. Being Queen is a big responsibility. You've made me so happy being here today."

Eve's mother places her hand on Eve's cheek and smiles. "You will never be alone my dear. I will be here for you. I have no doubt in my mind that you will make a great wife and have a wonderful family. My daughter has grown into a fine woman. I'm so proud of you."

"Mother, thank you. Please, tell me what your life was like after you were taken?"

"To be honest, it was love at first sight when I met my husband. He was kind and handsome. I felt a bond and connection that made my heart flutter. We now have two sons together. The Palace people are like family to me."

"I have brothers!"

Eve's mother laughs. "Yes, you do my dear. But you will always be my first born, my Royal child of Charles."

Eve smiles at her mother's words. "Your husband mother, does he know of me?"

"I did tell my husband about you. He was so understanding and was the one that decided to leave you with your father. My husband never told anyone about you. Funny thing is, he told me that one day I will see you again. Looks like he was right."

Eve and her mother continued their conversation about their lives until they heard a knock at the door. One of the guards opens the door.

"Queen Leona, your seats are ready."

"Eve, I must take my leave now. You look so beautiful; don't be nervous. You will do just fine. You're going to make a fine Queen. I will be watching this special moment."

Eve's mother gives her a kiss on her forehead and leaves the room. Eve stares at the door as her mother leaves. She remembers her father saying how much she looked like her mother. The only difference was that her mother's skin was a darker purple and her hair flowed down to her lower legs. Eve wishes her father could attend her wedding as well. She accepts that could never happen since her mother was present. As Eve was thinking, she was startled when she heard Ronzell burst through the door.

"Queeny, it's time, the wedding is starting."

Eve takes a deep breath and exhales. "I'm ready."

＊

Eve follows Ronzell to the ceremony. She peeks into the room where the guest was seated. There were Kings and Queens from every neighboring platform present. Her stomach begins to tense as her nerves kick in. She stops and remembers her mother's words. She is out there watching her special day. Eve glances over at Ronzell who gave her a wink and a smile. He has become another one of Eve's best friends. As her nerves calms down, she begins to walk down the aisle.

The maids were holding her long train as she walks. She looks around to see the guest smiling and whispering about how beautiful she looks. In the crowd she could see her mother and her family. Thoughts run through her mind about how happy they look. Her eyes eventually met up with Max who was taken by surprise by her beauty. His eyes were full of love and appreciation.

"Wow!" Max says in his mind. "I can't believe I was lucky enough to find such a woman. It feels like just yesterday I was saving her life and walking lost in the woods. She is truly about to be mine today. She's so kind and gentle hearted. I will do anything to make her happy."

Max reaches out his hand to Eve as she approaches. At that moment Max became speechless by her presence. His heart begins to beat faster as she stands in front of him. He leans in and whispers to her. "You know I almost died when you walked through those doors. You look breathtaking."

Eve blushes at his words and shyly smiles. The Elder shadow began to speak about how they will be bonded forever in love. He gets to the part of asking them the final question.

"Max, do you take Eve to be your wife for as long as you live?" The Elder asks with his echoing voice that sounds as if he was singing a sweet melody.

"I do."

"And do you Eve, take Max to be your husband for as long as you live?"

"I do."

"With the power bestowed upon me, I now pronounce you husband and wife. You may kiss your bride."

Max pulls Eve towards him and kisses her gently.

"All rise in welcoming a new King and Queen!"

The guest begins to clap and cheer as Max and Eve walk towards the exit.

The people and the guests of the Palace made their way towards the ballroom to witness the first dance of the newlyweds. Eve and Max make their way to the dance floor.

"Are you nervous about our first dance my lady?"

"Not when I'm with you."

"Then let us dance and enjoy this moment."

They began their first dance as King and Queen. Max spins and laughs with Eve as they enjoy each other's company. Eve looks in the distance of the room to see a hooded figure in the shadows. There in the corner of the room was a man she recognize.

"Father! How could this be?"

"That would be my doing my lady. I sent a message of our marriage across all the land and platforms. I gave a hidden message for your father to attend. I knew your mother would be here, so I took caution in keeping them separated. He won't be here long. He did thank me for allowing him to share this moment. Think of this as a wedding gift to you, my love."

Eve gives Max a long kiss. "Max, thank you, this is truly the greatest gift I could ever receive. I got a chance to have both my parents attend my wedding and see me become Queen. I love you with all my heart."

Eve looks over to her father smiling at her. He gives a small wave as she notices him. Eve felt as if her day was perfect. She continues to dance with Max a little longer. She glances back at the corner where her father stood to see he was no longer there. A small smile came across her face. That was more than enough time for her to see her father's presence. She knew he had to leave before he was in contact with her mother. His heart would weaken once more if that were to happen. This was everything she could ever ask for.

"Max?"

"Yes, my love?"

"What happens after the party is over?"

"Well, our honeymoon of course. I have many plans for you my dear, I hope your prepared for the love you're about to receive."

"Oh, I'm more than ready."

CHAPTER 15

THE HONEYMOON

After all the guests had taken their leave, Eve and Max make their way towards the ends of the Palace. The other end of the Palace felt different to Eve since there was barely anyone around. The atmosphere was calm and quiet. Eve feels as if she was entering an entirely new Palace. The walls and floor were white marble with swirling designs. Unlike the other side of the Palace, which had black flooring with red designs, this side felt pure and refreshing. There were beautiful spiral white pillars leading down the halls.

"This side of the Palace is much brighter. I'm enjoying the scenery."

"I'm glad you like it, my lady."

As they walk, Eve spots the end of the hall which had two large doors. Max stops in front of the large double doors with a design of two dragons facing each other. He opens the door for Eve and gestures for her to enter.

"We have arrived at our honeymoon suite, my lady."

Eve was a bit worried about how Max was acting. He had a Seductive vibe to him that made Eve a little nervous. When Eve walks in the room, she admires the astounding sight. Thinking to herself, she wonders how she could fit her entire house in this one room. There was a large kitchen area with an island stovetop in the middle of it. The living room area was designed with multiple white sofas and glass tables with white trimming. The room was filled with lovely pink candles with a bottle of wine with two glasses on the table. There was a glass slide door which led to the purple ocean outside. The stars glisten off the water's surface as the night sky darkens. A white stone patio was outside where they could sit and enjoy the view.

Eve saw there was a trail of red rose petals that was leading her into the bedroom. Their large maroon color bed was full of rare rose petals from the Shimmering Forest. She peeks in the bathroom to see a bubble bath waiting for her with candles around the rim. Eve was thinking that this was a night she was going to remember.

Max walks up behind her pulling her close to him. He kisses her soft lips as he holds her tight. Max was anxious about their night together. He never wanted her so badly.

"I will leave you to prepare for tonight my love. I will be in the bathing room next to this one and prepare as well."

"I must admit I'm a little nervous. I can't wait to spend this moment with you. I will be ready for tonight, Max."

Eve was left alone; she spotted a table with two letters and gifts on it. They were letters and gifts from her parents. The first letter was from her father. She takes a seat as she reads.

My Dearest Eve,

I was so happy to see you married to such a fine gentleman as Maximilian. I only spoke with him briefly, but I can see he truly loves you. He promised me that he would protect and love you for eternity. I feel as if I don't have to worry about my daughter anymore. I am sorry I couldn't stay longer than I would have liked to. I didn't want another setback. Seeing you in that gown left me with a memory I will forever cherish. I will try and come around occasionally to see you; I promise. Someday, you will have children of your own and I want to be there for them.

Love your father, Charles

Eve smiled after she finished reading the letter. She went on to open his gift which was wrapped in a red ribbon. There inside the box was a white moon flower jeweled bracelet.

"This material is so rare. How did father manage to get them? It is a lovely handmade bracelet. Father has always made things like this for me and my mother."

Eve was ready to read the next letter written by her mother.

To my lovely Daughter,

I'm so proud of you my dear. You are now a Queen of your own world. I know you will treat your people right and grow your platform. I told your brothers that you were their sister. I laughed when they were shocked about having a Queen for an older sister. They told me they wanted to get to know you some day, and so does my husband. Looks like you will be seeing more of us around. I can't wait to have some grandchildren. In your gift I gave you a little something that may help with that.

Love your dearest mother, Leona

Eve opens the gift that was wrapped with a blue ribbon. In this box was a white see-through gown with the back exposed. It had laced flowered trimming and matching tights that strapped to the see-through panty lingerie. She places a blue diamond necklace which is in its own ribbon box.

"Oh...my...gosh!"

Eve was observing the lingerie thinking how sexy this would look on her.

"This outfit will do more than help with baby making. I'm sure Max would love to see me in this. I never even wore anything like this before. Will I be able to pull something like this off? Well, there's only one way to find that out. Till then, I must prepare for tonight."

Eve takes her bath and slips on the gown and panties. She walked out of the room to see Max without a shirt on and a silk red velvety robe with undershorts. His mouth drops at the sight of Eve.

"So, do you like what I'm wearing?" Eve asks nervously.

Max bites his bottom lip and walks over to her. He pulls her close with force and begins to kiss her.

"I can't take this anymore. Eve, I'm going to make you scream my name tonight."

CHAPTER 16

A NIGHT OF PLEASURE

Max gently rubs down Eve's breast giving it a firm squeeze. His hands continue down her body causing it to tremble slightly. Max whispers in Eve's ear. "I can see how your body reacts to me. Looks like someone's looking forward to an exciting night."

"Um... I can explain..."

Max let out a small laugh. "No need to explain my dear. I have many plans for you tonight."

Max pushes Eve against the wall and nibbles on her ear while caressing her plump ass. He gives it a tight squeeze causing Eve to flinch. Her legs were beginning to weaken. She was ready to give herself to Max. He lifts Eve off the ground causing her to wrap her arms and legs around him. Eve moans as he kisses her while walking over to the bed. He lays Eve on the bed and rests between her thighs. Eve found herself staring at his strong muscle arms and six pack. It turned her on at the sight of his masculine body. She can feel his hard penis from his shorts as he lays between her.

"Hah...Max, I want you so bad right now."

"I've wanted you the moment I laid eyes on you, my love."

Eve thinks about how amazing Max is as he undresses her. Max takes his time feeling on Eve's perfect body.

"Your body is so perfect. Such soft and round breast; they sit just right on your body. Mmm... even your nipples are beginning to harden. I must taste you...all of you."

Max continues undressing her and begins to suck and play with Eve's nipples.

"Mmm... Max that feels amazing."

Eve began to stroke his hair while he licks and sucks her breast down to her stomach. He rolls his tongue around her stomach as he moves lower down her quivering body. Max made sure to take his time pleasing every inch of her body. He slowly removes her lingerie and kisses down to he reaches her already wet pussy. Eve grips the sheets as Max begins to eat her.

"Ah. Hah... Max I can hardly take what you're doing to me."

Max, moved by Eves words, begins to tighten his grip on Eve's thighs and pushes his tongue deeper inside her. Eve let out a moaning cry for Max to keep going. She pushes his head so that he may continue licking deep inside her. After eating her for a while, Max stops and stands to his feet licking the juiciness from his lips. He enjoyed driving Eve crazy causing her body to shake.

"How did you like that my love?" Max asks with a grin on his face.

"You, you are amazing." Eve says trying to catch her breath. "Now it's time I show you what I can do. I'm going to make you feel pleasure like never before."

"Oh yeah, please show me."

Eve removes Max's shorts and grips the base of his penis. She starts to stroke it up and down with a steady motion. Max let out a moan from her strokes. Eve begins to kiss the tip of his penis; she moans with every kiss she plants on it. Max's eyes start to roll as she pleases him.

"Hah... Eve, you're teasing me, I want so much more of this."

"Oh, there is more my King." Eve rolls her tongue around the tip of his penis. She licks him up and down slowly. Max let out a pleasing moan and balls his fist as Eve drives him crazy. Not wanting to tease any further, Eve begins to wrap her soft lips around his penis sucking and slurping him. Max grabs her hair and holds it into a ponytail.

"Eve, keep sucking, this feels so damn good."

Eve, loving Max's reaction, began to push her mouth forward so that Max was deeper into her throat. Max watches as his penis disappears into Eve's mouth. His eyes roll in his head as he faces the ceiling. He bites down on his lip trying to control his emotions. Eve continues to suck faster and faster.

"Eve! I can't hold it anymore if you keep sucking like this." Before he explodes, he pulls out of her mouth. He takes a deep breath and smiles at Eve.

"You really did please me. Now I will finish what I started."

Max lays Eve on her back and places the tip of his penis on her pussy. "Are you ready, my love?"

"Yes! Please Max don't tease me any further. I want you inside me."

Max lays between her as she wraps her arms and legs around him. He starts to kiss her as he slowly pushes his penis inside her. They both let out a moan.

"You are so wet."

"And you are so big. Please, continue."

Eve's nails began to scratch Max's back as he thrusts inside her. Unphased by her nails, Max begins to thrust harder. He took great pride in hearing his wife's moan.

"Oh, Max! Oh. Max! You are so amazing. It's so big, I love it!"

Eve's pussy was getting wetter as Max continues to make love to her. Max, feeling her wetness for too long, couldn't last any longer.

"Ah, Eve, I'm about to cum! You are even wetter than before; I can't take it."

Max releases himself deep inside of her. Eve let out a moan as she feels his warmth. Eve and Max's symbol of bonding love formed onto their backs as they finished. Max lay next to Eve as they both tried to catch their breath.

"Eve, I'm sorry, I wanted to go longer but you felt incredible. I couldn't help myself."

"No, that was amazing. I loved every moment of it. I feel like I truly belong to you now."

"I too, feel the same."

"Hey, would you like to go take a walk on the beach tomorrow?"

"We can do whatever you wish my lady."

Eve stares into Max's eyes loving everything about him. "I love you Max."

"I love you too Eve."

Max and Eve went to bathe and laid back with each other. They were both exhausted after their steamy night together. They cuddled up in the bed feeling the warmth of their bodies. Max gives Eve's forehead a kiss as they both start to drift off to sleep.

"What an amazing woman."

.

CHAPTER 17

NIGHT ON THE BEACH

Eve was excited about going to the beach. It was her first time seeing the ocean. She packs some lunch for her and Max to eat while they are out.

"Are you ready for our walk, my love?"

"Yes! I can't wait!"

They open the door to step outside. Eve can feel the soft breeze and smell the freshness of the ocean. It was a refreshing scent and lovely sight for Eve. The air had a different scent than when she was back in the village surrounded by the trees. She enjoys how clean the air feels. Max holds her hand as they start their walk. Suddenly they heard a loud crack and rumble in the sky. They look up to see a platform crumbling and falling apart.

"Oh No! Doesn't that mean?"

"Yes Eve. A Queen has died. And I have a feeling I know who could have caused it."

"The assassin?"

"Yes. Let us not think of that now. As irritating as it is, this is our honeymoon and I plan to enjoy every moment with you."

Eve smiles at Max. She knew that the sight of the crumbling platform was bothering him. She didn't want him to worry about her feelings nor his own. This was their night, and she didn't want it to be ruined.

"So Max, I was wondering about that day we met in the woods. Why was you out that day?"

Max let out a sigh, he looked to the sky. "Sad to say, but I was looking for the assassin that day."

"Darn it! I was trying to change the subject on that matter. I'm sorry I asked Max."

Max gave Eve a kiss on the hand. "Don't be so hard on yourself. I don't mind sharing my story with you."

"I had gotten word that the assassin might be on our world. So, I went out to search that day. I'm glad I did because I found you instead. I got a chance to meet the kindest and most beautiful woman I've ever laid eyes upon."

Max looks at Eve and smiles at her. Eve blushes and smiles shyly back at him.

Eve giggles. "I knew that day something was different about you. I was so attracted to everything about you."

"Oh, you were attracted to me huh. What was it you attracted too?"

Eve pauses and stares at Max. "Everything. Your voice, your touch, body, the way you handled the Alpha. I couldn't stop thinking of you and that night we shared our first kiss."

"I was having the same feeling. I was going mad without you. I thought I made a mistake leaving you behind that day. I trusted my love for you would lead me to be with you once more."

"The moment your hood fell off your head it shocked me. Not only were you a Royal born, but you were absolutely beautiful. The way your silky hair flowed and your gentle eyes glowed. I knew I had to have you as my wife. I remember you telling me you didn't stay far from the woods. It was sad how many villages that was destroyed trying to find you."

"What! What are you saying? Where innocent people killed while you searched for me?"

"Why yes Eve, those are the rules and laws of our worlds. As cruel as they may be. More villages are to be destroyed now that I have found you."

"No! It's not fair! Who made these laws anyway! They are cruel, I don't want to rule a world where people have to die."

Max stops walking and held onto Eve's chin. He didn't know that someone cares for the people the way she did. He understood her feelings.

"Maybe there's someone who can change the rules of the world. A brave Queen with a determine heart, perhaps." Max says as he stares into her eyes.

Eve stares back into Max's eyes. She was reminded of why she fell in love with him in the first place. She knows now from Max's words; she can change the laws of this world. She would bend the rules if she had too.

"Thank you, Max. Your words have spoken to my heart."

She pulls Max closer and kisses him with great passion.

"My pleasure, my love. I will do anything to help you change the rules."

"I know you will."

Both continue their walk until Eve's stomach begins to rumble. "I am starving. Are you ready to eat?"

"I am rather hungry myself. Let's stop here for the night."

They sat under the moons and stars on the soft blanket Max packed and began to eat.

"This is perfect. Maybe this should've been where we had our first date." Eve says with a giggle.

"I should have considered it."

As Eve and Max conversate, off in the distance they heard a loud roar.

"A shadow bear!" Eve shouted. "What's it doing out here? What's going on? Why is all this happening today of all days?"

"It must of came from those woods over in the distance." Max replied.

There stood an 8-foot shadow bear with its body as wide as a wagon. It had red glowing eyes and fangs about 4 inches long. Its fur stands upright as it prepares to attack.

"Eve! Stand back! I won't allow this beast to get close to you."

Max began to manifest his dark flaming wings with a dark blue rim light around them. His wings were like a shadow bird. He extended his claws, and his eyes glowed a brighter purple than before. Eve feels the pressure of Max's dragon powers. Before she can blink, she feels a gush of wind from Max as he rushes towards the shadow bear.

Eve watches as Max flies around the shadow bear. "What incredible speed he has."

The bear stands upright on its back legs and swipes at Max. Max dodges with ease as fast as he was flying. He claws at the bear's stomach slicing it open. Max flies behind the beast's head and grabs hold of it. Max spins the head of the bear 360 degrees. The bear made a loud thud as it hit the ground. Eve's eyes were wide as she witnessed the strength of her husband. She was frightened by the murderous look Max gave off. Max frowns as he looks at the dead bear. His hands were covered with blood.

"He looks as if killing was nothing to him." Eve thought to herself. "I can see why the Alpha ran off that day. If I had seen Max's face looking the way it is now, I would have surely ran too."

Max walks over to the ocean to clean the blood from his hands. "Eve, are you alright my dear? You look frighten."

"Um…no, I was just surprised at your strength. What about you, are you ok?"

"I am Fine. The thought of that bear harming you made me angry. I couldn't imagine what would happen if anything ever happened to you. I will never let anyone, or thing hurt you."

Eve touches Max cheek gently. She speaks softly to him. "I am fine Max. I know you will always protect me. Don't stress yourself."

Max's body calms as Eve speaks to him. He releases his flaming wings and retracts his claws.

"So, I think I have had enough of the beach for one night." Eve says with a smile. "This was an interesting walk right Max?"

Max let out a chuckle. "That it was, my love. Let us gather the meat and fur from the bear and head back. I will cook him for us for dinner tonight."

"Um, no. I don't think I will ever eat that thing." she says pointing at the bear.

"What do you mean my love?" Max asks with confusion. "You loved it so much last time you ate it."

Eve frowns at Max. "What do you mean, last time?"

"Well, on our first date, you said you loved the steak I cooked. You said you could eat it forever. That was shadow bear steak."

"You…you fed me shadow bear meat for our first date!"

"Yes, my love. You said it was the best food you have ever eaten."

Max was clearly messing with Eve at this point. He thought she was cute the way she complains. He couldn't help but to keep teasing her on the matter.

"It was the best meat you ever had right?"

"Well not the best meat." Eve said with a wink.

"Oh my, aren't you a naughty one."

Eve blushes a little as she looks at Max. "Let's get back. You are going to cook me this bear and then I'm going to bed."

"As you wish my love."

CHAPTER 18

MORNING WOOD

The next morning, Eve wakes to a stunning view of the bright purple ocean as it sparkles. She sees the waves brushing up against the sands and the shadow whales on the ocean's surface.

"What a lovely sight. Even though last night's walk got a little scary I still enjoyed myself. It was great being on the sandy shore for the first time."

Eve looks over to Max lying beside her. She smiles happily knowing she can spend her life with such a wonderful husband. She felt as if her world had changed in the best way.

"I'm so lucky. Just look at how hot he is. He does nothing but make me feel safe and comfortable."

Her eyes began to drift admiring her husband's body. She couldn't help but crave his hard penis which was poking up from the sheets.

"I can't resist I must have him again." She began stroking his penis as she gently kisses his neck.

"Mmm...Eve that feels good."

"I'm sorry. Your penis was so hard I couldn't help but touch and play with it."

"Oh really. Then allow me to return the favor."

Max rolls to his side and begins to rub on Eve's pussy. Eve let out a moan as he began kissing and sucking her neck. He pulls her to the edge of the bed spreading her legs. He tightens his grip around her ancles so that she couldn't run from him.

"I won't be holding back on you, my love. I hope you are ready for what you've started."

Max pushes his penis inside her and start to pound her aggressively.

"Ah, ah, Max!"

Max continues to accelerate his speed pounding her harder than before. "You like the way I'm pounding you don't you Eve?"

"Hah…yes! I love it! Harder, harder!"

Max pushes Eve's legs until they reached her head and continues thrusting her as hard as he could. Her pussy became wetter with every thrust. Eve begins to climax as she feels him take control of her body.

"Max! You are the Greatest!"

"I'm going to cum so hard in you Eve!"

"Yes! I want to feel your warmth inside me Max."

Max let out a pleasing moan as he fills Eve with his cum. Eve exhales as he slowly pulls out of her.

"Wow that felt amazing Max. You were much harder now than the first time we did it."

"I tend to be hard every morning." Max says, giving Eve a wink.

"Every morning? I'm so looking forward to mornings now."

Max laughs at her words. "I will be looking forward to it as well, my love."

"So, um, I guess we are finish right?"

"Who told you we were finish?" Max says with a confused look on his face.

"Wait! What are you saying?"

Eve felt like she couldn't handle any more of Max's sex. Max could see Eve was nervous about going another round. Her body was still trembling. He couldn't help his feelings and wanted to feel more of Eve. His body was craving more as he was still horny. He grabs her wrist and pulls her up towards him. He turns her around and nibbles on her ear as he squeezes her firm breast. Eve loves when he breathes in her ear. Her eyes roll as he fondles her body.

He bends her forward and slides inside of her. He spanks and squeezes her ass as he pounds her once more. Eve's breathing becomes heavy as she enjoys his dominance.

"I thought...hah... you couldn't go another round. How are you doing this?"

Max ignores her questions as he was focusing on pleasing her body. He leans forward and wraps his hand around her neck and whispers in her ear.

"This is our honeymoon, and I will be pleasing you every day until it's over."

He breathes heavy into her ear as he strokes her from behind. Eve feels as if she was going to pass out. Her body was vibrating out of control. Max stops and lets her rest for a moment. He picks her up and walks to the shower. Max enjoys watching the water fall down Eve's curvy body. He began to suck and drink the water flowing off Eve's breast. Max picks up her wet body and leans her against the glass. Once again inside her he begins to thrust her slowly.

"Max! I can't take any more of this! My legs…they are so shaky I can barely stand."

Max ignores Eve and continues to stroke her wet body. Eve couldn't take much more of him. Max holds her legs tightly around his hips and continues his slow thrust. Eve's moans began to flutter as she tried to catch her breath. Max was pushing her body to its limits. She moans loudly as he kisses and bounces her up and down. Eve begs for him to stop as she can no longer take it. Max, not being able to handle her wetness any longer releases hard inside of her. He breathes heavily as he slides her back down to her feet.

Max smiles at Eve as her body continues to vibrate and twitch. Eve found herself speechless for a moment. She stares at Max appreciating the love he has for her.

Eve lays on Max's chest and holds him. "I will never leave your side. I promise to love you for eternity."

"You know I will love you for all eternity as well, my love."

"This has been the best honeymoon so far. I can't wait to see where our future takes us Max. What are our plans after our honeymoon is over?"

"Well, my love, you are going to go train. You must learn to control your flames and building skills. This platform has potential to be one of the grand platforms if built correctly. If you want to change the laws of this world than we need to make a statement that we mean business."

"Ok, easy enough. Who will I be training with?"

"My head guardsman Garret."

"Oh, you've got to be kidding me!"

CHAPTER 19

TRAINING DAY

Both Eve and Max had returned to the main part of the Palace. They were greeted by the guards and the maids. They bow their heads as Eve and Max enter the main halls of the Palace.

"Welcome home my King and Queen." The guards and maids say.

"Is this how we are always going to be greeted?"

"Well yes, most of the time. This is how they show their respect. You will get accustomed to it my love."

Eve looks up to see Ronzell running straight for her. He squeezes her tight in his arms. "Ooh how I missed you Queeny." Ronzell says in a wining voice. "You must tell me all about your honeymoon."

Eve let out a laugh. "Ronzell, it hasn't been that long. I've only been gone a couple of weeks. Plus, I can't tell you everything about my honeymoon."

Eve looks over to Max and shyly blushes. Ronzell shoots Eve a little wink as he caught on to what she was saying.

"Eve! You naughty girl."

"Wait, Ronzell, I um, well you see…"

"Say no more I get what you were doing. Besides that, I've been missing our little talks we use to have. I have been bored to death without you. While you were gone, I've been working like crazy designing you the most fabulous dresses. You must try them on."

Eve smiles at Ronzell's actions. He was one of her best friends and had made her feel comfortable ever since she arrived at the Palace. She was looking forward to all the gossip she knew he had for her.

"Ronzell, thank you for making me lovely dresses. I will be happy to try them on for you."

"Oh Queeny, you are the best!"

"My Love, I'm happy to see you and Ronzell chat about your future plans. Right now, we have matters to attend. I must escort you to the training area."

"Oh great, do I have to train with Garret?"

Eve rolled her eyes and folded her arm with disapproval. Max let out a laugh as he loves seeing her get all pouty.

"Yes, my love, He is the very best at combat and knows how to train Royals. I wouldn't trust any other with your training than Garret. He trained me when I was a child."

"He's still a big fat jerk. He was mean to my friends and threatened my village."

"My love, I made sure that Garret took whatever measures necessary to find and bring you to me. If anyone is to blame for his actions, it would be me."

Eve let out a wining cry. She knew she could never be angry with Max. Max grabs Eve's chin and pulls her close for a kiss.

"You are so adorable when you are all pouty. It's starting to turn me on. You might want to reconsider your actions, or I may be forced to punish you."

Eve whispers in his ear. "Maybe I do need a little punishment."

"How about when I get back from my duties?"

"Sounds good to me. For now though, let's get my training over with."

"Good girl. You will be fine."

Max escorts Eve to the outside training ground. Garret stops what he was doing and runs up to them.

"Hello my King. My Queen, allow me to reintroduce myself. I am Sir Garret Grondell, head guardsman of the Shadow Knights. You may also know us as your Royal guards. I will be your personal trainer.

"Well, it is nice to meet you." Eve says taking a deep breath.

Eve was trying not to be irritated by Garret's presence. She wanted to show Max that she could be civilized. All she could remember was that day Garret was threatening her friend August and the villagers. The event left Eve feeling bitter towards Garret and the other guards. She thought about the guard who tried to sleep with her the day before her wedding. She wonders how she could trust guards as cruel as they were.

"Garret I will be leaving now. I leave my wife in your care. Make sure she is safe at all costs.

"I will make sure to take care of the Queen. I will show her around the training area."

Garret turns around so that he may lead Eve to start her training. Eve rolls her eyes as he walks away. Max, seeing her actions, gave her a smack on the ass and a wink. Eve turns and smiles. She knew he was telling her to be nice to Garret. She went on to follow and meet up with him on the training ground.

"Here is where we will start first my Queen. We will start small training to get you warmed up for more intense training later."

"Okay, that sounds fair. What do you want me to do?"

"We will start with running three laps."

"Three laps that's all. I used to run all the time back in the village. This should be easy."

"Now, let's begin our laps around the Palace." Garret says proudly.

"Around the.. do you realize how huge this Palace is!"

Garret puts his hands on his hips and grins at Eve. "I have no doubt in my mind that you can finish these laps my Queen."

Eve frowns at Garret and squints her eyes at him. "Oh, I get it, you're trying to kill me, aren't you?"

Garret, feeling panicky, kneels and bows his head. "My Queen! I would never try such a thing!"

Eve was a little shocked by his actions. "Wait, Garret! It was only a joke. I didn't really think you were out to kill me."

Garret rises from the ground and puts his hands on his hips. "Oh, a joke. Ha ha ha, good one my Queen. You got me there; I thought you would seriously think I would cross you or the King. My Queen, I swear to you on my life, that I will never betray you. I will protect you and your future children with my life. If anyone dares to defy you, I will destroy them."

Eve was pleased with Garrets actions. She can see in his eyes his dedication and loyalty to her and Max. There was a reason that Max spoke so highly of him. She could sense that Garret would never harm her or her family. He had the presence of a protective father that she never would have noticed before. Eve knew she had to be honest about how she felt about him.

"Garret there is something I need to get off my chest. I... I didn't like you at first. You came to my village ready to burn and harm the people who I see as my family. You threatened one of my best friends, August. I believed you to be a horrible person. Plus, that guard that attacked me that night, he was one of your men."

Garret stares at Eve for a moment. "First my Queen let me apologize for that guard ever attacking you. I know all my men and he was new to the Palace. I won't make any excuses; I should have read his vibes better. If I am allowed to stay your head Guard, then I promise I will never have men serve under me that would harm you or any woman. The King and I dealt with the situation, and this will never happen again. I promise."

"I believe you Garret." Eve says softly. "I can tell you are a man worth trusting."

Garret let out a hard laugh.

"What so funny?"

"Well, that explains every time you see me you roll your eyes and frown at me. I felt a little attitude when I reintroduced myself as well."

"Oh, you've notice that." she says nervously.

"I notice almost everything. I'm the best at reading others. That is why I am still alive."

Eve and Garret start to walk around as they were getting to know each other.

"I also notice that you are a kindhearted person. It takes courage to stand up for what you believe in my Queen. Anyone willing to stand up to an army for the people she cares about is someone I will gladly give my life for. I was excited when the King entrusted me to train you."

"You were?"

"Yes. I enjoy training Royals. I've fought beside the Kings father on the battlefield and promised I would help train his son. Training the Dragon King as a child was quite exciting. He was so eager to try new things. When he learned to manifest his wings there was no stopping him. I know him for being the fastest Royal King I have ever met. He is also the strongest King I know other than the 1st Dragon King."

"Funny you should mention that. I was able to see his strength on the beach a couple of weeks ago. He fought and killed a shadow bear that was trying to attack us."

"A shadow bear! Out here! Where did it come from?"

"Max believes it came from the woods behind the Palace."

"I shall see to it that my men scout the area for any more of them."

"That would put my mind at ease knowing the people of the Palace would be safe." Eve says with a smile.

"You see, that's why I want to train you. You are always putting others first. I respect that. I need you to be able to protect yourself as well my Queen."

"I understand Garret."

"Did I forget to mention that you would be the first Royal Queen I've ever trained. I want someone like you with such courage and passion to be great."

"Garret, thank you for all your kind words. Are you trying to get on my good side or something?"

"It depends, did my words make you trust me?"

"Yeah, I guess you're alright." Eve says, giving Garret a pat on the back.

Eve thought she could never imagine someone like Garret could be such a gentle giant. He may be a muscled man built for the battleground, but he had a kind and loyal heart. She wonders why he was so aggressive the day she was being taken.

"Garret, that day you and your men arrived, why did you have to be so aggressive? You could have been compassionate, like you are now."

"I was just doing my job. I also saw your friend as someone trying to stop the Queen from marrying the Dragon King. The action alone was treason to the Palace and the laws of the worlds. Because he was your friend, and you gave yourself up willingly I let him live. Shall he pull something like that again I'm afraid I will have to take proper action against him."

"That is fair. The way I feel for Max, I wouldn't want anyone to interfere. Thanks anyway for sparing my friend big guy."

"My pleasure, my Queen. Now shall we get on with running our laps. I need to build your stamina."

"Oh Shoot! The laps! I was hoping you forgot about it." Eve says in a whining voice.

"Ha ha ha ha, nope. Let's get to running my Queen."

CHAPTER 20

ONE THING AFTER ANOTHER

Eve runs the entire three laps with Garret and collapses at the finish line.

Huff... huff… "Are we done running yet?" Eve asks while trying to catch her breath.

"Yes, my Queen, we are done for today seeing that you are extremely tired. We will pick up where we left off and run another three laps tomorrow."

"I knew it! You really are trying to kill me."

Garret let out a laugh seeing that Eve must be joking again.

Eve was escorted back to the Palace to rest for more training tomorrow. She flops in the bed and falls fast asleep before Max ever returns.

The next day Eve continues to run with Garret. Exhausted from the run, Eve was thinking that her body felt as if it was breaking and getting stronger at the same time. She still felt like something was off with how exhausted she was.

"I knew I would be tired, but this feeling is strange."

Garret stops running seeing how tired Eve looked. He thought it would be best if they took a short break. He starts to conversate with her about the rest of her training while they rest.

"It looks like you are doing better today. You still seem a bit tired so let's start with something else. Let's talk about your flames and building skills."

"What about them?"

"Well, as Queen you must know how to morph the lands and create knew things. Your flames are used for protecting yourself and others. We must practice using both of your abilities. You may choose to create a new platform or choose this one since no other Queen has claimed it. This decision is entirely your choice."

Eve thought for a moment about such a serious decision. "I think, I will choose this world as my own."

"Magnificent choice my Queen! Now that you have chosen a platform, you may morph and construct on it as you please. You can take any piece of the land, water, even trees and duplicate it. You may bend, and even shrink them if you like. It's your world. Let's try something small for now, like that stone over there. Focus your powers and envision what you want it to be."

Eve closes her eyes and takes a deep breath. She focuses her energy on the rock before her, it starts to move and take shape until it splits into two stones.

"Wow! I did it! But..."

Eve suddenly feels dizzy. As she starts to fall Garret reaches out to catch her.

"My Queen you should be alright. This should be normal for your first attempt. This is why I wanted you to build your stamina. It takes a lot of focus and energy to build the lands."

Eve suddenly had a new appreciation for all the Queens out there creating and building their lands. Garret hands Eve some water and sits her down.

"My Queen, your flames work in the same way as your building skills. You can shape your flames to be whatever you want. You can make a sword, bows, spears, whatever you can imagine them to be. But for now, you need to go rest, you look oddly drained. Maybe I should take you back to the Palace for now."

Eve was escorted to her room as she became weaker.

"Well, you are home early my lady." Max says.

She was startled when she heard Max's voice. "Max! You caught me off guard for a moment."

Eve walks over to her husband and kisses him. "What are you doing here? I thought you had business to attend."

"I did. I thought I would take some time to come see how my wife is doing with her training. Plus, I can't keep my mind from thinking about you."

Max grabs Eve's hips and pulls her close to him. He begins kissing her passionately. Eve let out a small moan as he kisses her.

"I have been thinking of you as well. You may be happy to hear that me and Garret are friends now. I finally got to tell him why I was so angry with him. He went on to tell me his side of the story and how his loyalty is to us. He's a good man and I can see why you trust him."

"I am so proud of you, my love. You were able to make up with Garret. I knew you just needed some time to get to know him."

"Yeah, I'm glad I did."

"Have you decided where we are going to live?"

"I have chosen to create on this world."

"Excellent choice, I knew you would. I'm so delighted to hear that. I have a bit of attachment to this world as well, since this is where my father placed me before he died. We can talk about our future plans later though. Right now, I need you."

Max starts to kiss and undress Eve at that moment.

"Max! What are you doing? Don't you have to get back to your business?"

"Yes, but I need you right now, I can't focus if I'm horny for you. It will just be a quick one I promise."

"Okay fine, I've wanted you too. Let's try not to let anyone hear us, okay."

"My love, this is our home, we can be as loud as we want."

He continues to undress Eve and mounts her on top of his penis. She leans forward to kiss him as she grinds on him slowly.

"Hah…Max this feel so good."

"You feel wetter than ever Eve. I don't want you to stop riding me."

Max and Eve's breathing became heavier as she rode him harder. He grips her hips tightly so that he may bounce her on is hard penis. He starts to smack, squeeze, and dig his claws into her ass.

"Eve, you are just so wet I can't handle this anymore. I'm going to release so hard inside of you."

They both moan as he releases inside of her. Max laid back to relax as Eve was still on top of him.

Max grins at Eve. "See now that didn't take anytime at all. Now we can both focus on our work."

"You really are naughty. But I really need to rest, I feel more drained than ever before."

"Did Garret push you too hard in your training today?"

"No, Garret has been really understanding when it comes to how much I can handle. I morphed a stone today and did some running."

"Hmm…Well that's strange. Was it a large stone you morphed?"

"No, more like a medium size one."

"Well, that shouldn't have you in this condition. I will call for Ronzell and the Doctor to have you checked out. I want to be safe about what's going on with you."

"Sure, my love. The way I'm feeling just doesn't seem right."

***

Later that evening, Eve was sent to bed rest. She hears someone complaining down the hall. Before she knew it, Ronzell came bursting through the doors.

"Oh Queeny, what has that Garret done to you?" Ronzell says in a whining tone. "He worked you too hard, didn't he?"

Ronzell places his hands on his hips and turns to frown at Garret.

"Ronzell, calm down, it's not Garret's fault. I'm just experiencing some fatigue is all."

As Ronzell begin to protest, a tall well-dressed male of white hair walks through the door. He had a very gentle voice and was quite handsome. He had dark grey skin and a well-toned body. He was born of the medical shadow race. They have powers to heal anything and sense whatever is wrong in one's body. They are always born with beautiful snowy white hair. Eve was thinking that he would be Luna's type of guy to marry. Thinking of Luna put Eve's mind at ease. She was hoping that nothing was seriously wrong with her.

"Well, it seems to be very lively in this room." The Doctor says. "My name is Dr. Lotus. I am one of the highest ranked medical healers known. If you don't mind my Queen, I would like to check to see what is wrong with you. Please just relax and lay back for me. This examination will only take a moment."

Dr. Lotus hovers his hands over Eve's body. They glowed a bright green color. It was warm and soothing to Eve.

"Well, I have found the issue here. First let me begin by saying she can no longer train for a while."

"I knew it! You have been training my Queeny to hard Garret!"

Garret went into a panic. "My King I swear I was very mindful of how much the Queen could handle. I would never want any harm to come to her."

"I believe you Garret. Now let the doctor finish what he has to say."

Dr. Lotus let out a laugh at all the drama that was happening in the room.

"So, doctor." Eve says in a gentle tone. "What's wrong with me?"

"Nothing's wrong with you, my Queen."

"Then how do you explain her condition?" Ronzell says, interrupting the doctor. "Are you sure you are the best medical doctor?"

"Ron…Zell!" Eve says aggressively. "Will you stop interrupting and let him finish talking."

"Yes, ma'am." Ronzell says in a softer tone.

"Alright I will explain the issue. My Queen, you will have more work on your hands for the future. This is because you, are pregnant."

"She's Pregnant!" They all shout.

CHAPTER 21

NO TIME TO REST

"Doctor." Eve says in shock. "Are you sure? I'm…I'm pregnant?"

"Yes, you are. Your pregnancy was the reason you have been feeling so drained. It wouldn't be healthy for you if you continued to morph any of the lands or use your flames. You can cause some serious harm to yourself and your unborn children."

"Children!" They all shout.

Dr. Lotus chuckles. "You guy's reactions are so funny. The answer to your question is yes, you are pregnant with twins."

"Oh, my, gosh!" Ronzell says with excitement. "I can't wait to hold these little ones and dress them in my best designs. I have so much work ahead of me. I must fix the nursery, make their clothes, oh this is fantastic!"

"Calm yourself Ronzell. You don't want to overwhelm my wife, do you?"

"Oh, sorry your Majesty, I might have gotten a little over excited."

"A little excited in an understatement." Eve says under her breath.

"So, doctor how far along is my wife?"

"She is about four weeks. She will have another three months before the babies are born."

Eve starts to wonder off in her thoughts. She was thinking how sudden this was to her. She came to realize that she was about to start her own family. Max walks over to her seeing how concerned she looked.

"Are you alright my love? You seem to be lost in thought."

Eve looks at Max with her cute frowny face. "This is all your fault Max." she whispers.

"Well of course it is my love, I take full responsibility for this situation."

Eve stares at Max while he laughs at the situation. She couldn't find herself to be mad at him. He was the love of her life, and she was happy to start a family with him. Eve could tell that he was genially happy. Her thoughts were interrupted by Garret as he suddenly put his fist to his chest and apologize.

"My Queen, if I had known you were pregnant, I would have never started your training. I pushed you too hard and it could have cost you your life and the life of your unborn children."

"Garret, you didn't do anything wrong. No one could have seen this coming. Even with all the sex, I mean, all the time me and Max spent together I am just as surprise about the news. I am glad to know that all of you will be by my side as I go through this pregnancy. Just give me some time to take in all these events."

Max and Dr. Lotus let out a small laugh after Eve almost spilled the information about the sex she and Max was having. Max was still amazed and proud of the news. He was thinking of the new chapter that's about to begin for him and his new wife.

"If you don't mind the interruption my dear, I would like to present a gift to you that I have been eager to give you. I was going to give this to you before I found out you were pregnant. Now seems like a proper time. This should also put your mind at ease from all the events you've endured these past weeks."

"Haven't you already eagerly given me your gift already?" Eve says gesturing at her belly.

Max couldn't help but laugh at her joke. "Well, that is one gift I am very proud of. This gift that I have instore for you is something I believe you will appreciate."

Max snaps his fingers for the maids to bring in Eve's gift. They walk in holding a beautiful cat owl bird. Eve looks over from her bed in disbelief. Cat owl birds are one of the rarest birds on the platforms of each world. They are loyal and the most gorgeous breed bird known to the shadow people. The bird stood about three feet high and two feet wide. Its fur and wings were black with a glowing blue trim around the wings and edges of its fur. It has a fluffy catlike face with glowing pearly blue eyes. The body was that of a shadow owl with wings as soft as the fur on its face. Its face looks like one of the small shadow cats the people adore.

"This is the most beautiful bird I have ever seen. Is this bird really mine?"

"Yes, she is your very own message bird. She can travel to and from platform to platform. They are known to have incredible speed and stamina. She can find and message anyone you like if you present a scent to her. I know she will be of great use to you."

"Max, Thank you! This is an amazing gift. I can message my mother and even my father now. I can even message my friends."

"I'm glad you like it my love."

Eve reaches out to Max's face and pulls him in for a kiss. "You truly are the best."

"You do tell me that all the time." Max says with a wink.

Eve tries not to blush at his words. He knew just what to say to make her smile and laugh.

"Now, you need to eat plenty of food and rest." Max says. "You shouldn't strain yourself or do anything too dramatic for the next three months. You already know how deadly pregnancy can be. You wouldn't want me putting Ronzell on your bedrest duty, do you?"

"Oh, please don't Max!"

"I will be happy to do the job my King!" Ronzell says in a proudful way.

"Garret you are to guard me from Ronzell. You know how he gets."

"I will do my best my Queen."

"Garret can't stop me from doing my job. I will be here every night to make sure you are following the doctor's orders Queeny."

Eve's eyes start to water as she looks at Max. "You're going to pay for this Max." she whispers.

"I'll make it up to you later my love."

Max gestures for everyone to leave Eve alone to rest. Soon as everyone left the room, Eve felt that she couldn't rest now. She had other plans in mind first. She reaches out to rub the fur on her bird's head. The cat owl birds fur calms Eve's nerves as she thinks.

"I must give you a name don't I girl."

The cat owl let out a purring meow.

"Let's see, how about, Meela."

The cat owl purrs louder and let out a meow of approval.

Eve giggles at her new furry friend. "I guess you like that name don't you. Well, I have a job for u to do for me. Meela. I need you to send a letter to my friend Luna."

Eve begins writing the letter. Soon after she finished, she presents Meela with the scent of Luna. She takes off the bracelet that Luna had made for her and allows Meela to sniff it. Eve ties the letter to the foot of Meela.

"You're all set Meela." She gives her a kiss on the head and watches her fly out the window.

"Be safe out there Meela." she says softly. "As the new Queen, I am going to bend the rules and laws of our world. Starting with saving as many villagers as possible."

CHAPTER 22

A JOB FROM THE QUEEN

Back in the village, Luna was out in the fields picking veggies for her dinner. She looks to the sky to see a shadow bird with a blue glow coming from it.

"What on the worlds is that?" Luna was almost frightened by the figure as it flew towards her at high speed. It landed next to her and meowed.

"Wow! A cat owl bird! I have only seen one of these before, a white one if I recall."

Luna saw that the bird had a letter attached to its foot. She walks slowly towards the bird hoping it won't attack her. She opens the letter and starts to read.

"It's a letter from Eve! This must be her message bird. I haven't heard from her in weeks. I wonder what she is doing in her new life."

Dear Luna,

I know you are going to be shocked at the sight of my message bird. My husband got it for me so that I may contact my loved ones. Her name is Meela. She's very sweet so don't be afraid. Let me start by saying how much I miss you, August, and the people of our village. I hope you are all doing well.

As you know, I am the Queen now. It seems like just yesterday I was hiding my identity in the village. I see that didn't last as long as I would have liked it to be. I do like it here in the Palace, the people are like family to me and help me through my problems. My husband has been so supportive. I love him with all my heart. I know you're going to be shocked to hear this, but I am pregnant. I am pregnant with, well, twins. It was a shock to me as well but it's ok. I am madly in love with their father and wouldn't have it any other way. Oh, and the doctor here is so handsome and just your type. Maybe you will get to meet him one day.

The day of my wedding I was able to be reunited with my mother. She has a beautiful family now and I know she will teach me how to be a great mother. My father was also there and alive. It brought me joy that day.

This isn't the only reason I am sending you this letter, Luna. Now that I have caught you up to speed, I have a very important job that I can only trust you with. This task will send you on a long journey, I hope you will be able to accept it. I need you to travel the lands and gather up as many villages as possible and bring them to our village to live. The Law states they will have to die if they are not from my home. I don't want any more bloodshed on my world if I am to be Queen.

I want you to tell the people, I the Queen, want them to live. They must hurry before it is too late. I will feel better knowing that we can save as many people as possible.

Please Luna, can you do this for me? Will you help me save the people? Are you willing to do this not only for your Queen but for your friend, your sister at heart? I'm counting on you girl; I know you won't let me down.

Love you always, Eve

Luna stood staring at the letter with her mouth wide. She was overjoyed by Eve's letter. What was shocking to her was that Eve was pregnant with twins. She thinks about how Eve hadn't changed and was still the same kindhearted person she had always known. Eve trusts her to carry out a task to save the people. She always remembered how Eve would take care of anyone in need.

"Wow, I am so happy for her. She also has a handsome doctor too. Eve knows how I love the medical clan. They are so hot. Maybe I could meet him. Well, I need to stay focused on the main objective. Eve trusts me to carry out this mission. I will go to August's place and give him the news. I'm sure he wouldn't mind going on a little adventure with me. Especially if it's a task from Eve."

Luna rushes over to August place. "August! August are you home?"

"Luna what is wrong?"

"Nothing's wrong. Look, it's a letter from Eve. It was sent by Eve's cat owl bird."

August reads the letter and frowns angrily upon it. "What is Eve thinking! She's even pregnant by that man she barely even knows! She's only been in the Palace for some weeks and now this!"

"August! What has gotten into you? I thought you would be happy to hear from Eve after what has happened. She is happy and safe in the Palace. She is still the same person trying to protect and save the people."

"You are not actually going to go through with this mission?"

"Yes August! I was hoping you would come on this journey with me, but I can see you don't even care."

"So, we are supposed to risk our lives going on some dangerous journey while she sits in safety in her Palace. What did they do, brainwash her or something? I thought she wanted to live a normal life. We are supposed to be a family."

"Things change August. And we are still a family. Eve has a responsibility as Queen of this world. Don't you want to help her save the other villagers?"

"The other villagers are not my problem."

Luna slaps August in the face. "How could you say such words August! Do you not remember the day the Royal guards came to burn and kill the people if Eve wasn't present? Do you remember the fear we all felt when we thought we were going to die? That is what Eve is trying to prevent for the other villages. I am happy to have a Queen and friend who cares for us the way she does. Rather you come or not, I'm going to help Eve save the people.

Luna turns and walks away. "Goodbye August."

Later that day Luna starts packing her bags for the long journey ahead. August walks up to her.

"So, you're just going to leave too just like Eve did."

Luna ignores him and climbs onto her wagon. She began her journey into the woods never looking back.

"I've had enough of this!" August says aggressively. "I will take matters into my own hands if I must. It's time I hired that assassin I've been hearing about for our dear King and his stupid head guardsman. I will have my family back."

CHAPTER 23

<u>UNEXPECTED GUEST</u>

Off in the distant part of the lands, a man had cube warped to Eve's world.

"I made it." The man says. "Looks like I might be here for a while. According to this map, I need to head straight through those woods to reach my destination."

On the other side of the same woods Luna was making her way down the trail. She happens to hit a large bump in the road which causes the back of her wagon door to swing open. All of Luna's luggage came crashing down out of the back.

"Oh great, you have got to be kidding me! This is the worst of luck. My bags could have fallen out anywhere else. Instead, they fell while I'm deep within these scary woods of all places."

Luna walks around to see how much of her luggage has fallen out. She sighs as she picks up her bags in a hurry.

"I still remember when Eve, August, and I were attacked by those shadow wolves. I still have nightmares of that horrible day. Maybe if I hurry, I won't have to encounter them again. I don't have my friends this time. Maybe if August was here, I wouldn't be afraid."

Luna was thinking about the fight she and August had had the day before she left. They never fought like that before. She hopes they can make up when she returns home. Luna thought how she was beginning to have special feelings for him and didn't want that to be ruined by their argument. Thoughts continue to run through her mind as she continues to pick up her bags.

Closer to Luna's location the mysterious man was approaching. "Looks like it's just a little further." The man says.

As he hops from tree to tree, he comes across Luna struggling with her bags.

Luna didn't even realize the man staring at her from the trees above as she throws her heavy luggage onto the wagon.

"Well, well, well. What do we have here? A woman alone in these woods, how strange. Any woman who is brave enough to step foot in these woods alone is either crazy or they have somewhere important to be. I wonder what's her story."

The man watches Luna for a bit as she bends over to grab her bags.

"Wow! Look at the ass on her. I wasn't looking for a wife on my journey but there is something I find attractive about this woman. She is beautiful and looks as if she can handle her own. Those curves, her breast, and hips, I must talk to her."

The man hears strange movements coming from the shadows of the woods. He looks down to see that Luna was being stalked by the stalker of the woods.

"Oh no, a shadow wolf! It's going to attack her!"

Luna was about to place another one of her bags on the wagon when she heard a massive growl behind her. The shadow wolf leaps towards her. Before the Wolf could get close, the mysterious man jumps down from the trees kicking the wolf in the side. It made a loud cry as it fell to the ground. Before it could stand, the man moves faster than Luna could keep up with and sliced the wolf's throat.

Luna was lost for words. She stares at the man who had just saved her life. He turns to look at her. Luna was charmed by the man as she stares into his eyes. The man was tall with dark blue slick back hair and low shaved sides. His eyes were sharp and fierce. He was wearing a dark brown brim hat and a long dark brown trench coat. His pants were made of leathery cloth with a pair of boots that looked easy to run in. Luna was extremely attracted to him.

"Who is this man?" Luna asks in her mind. "He came out of nowhere. Well, I'm glad he did, or I may be dead right now. Look at his smile, he is so damn sexy. I can see his muscles and abs showing from his tight shirt. The look of this man rivals the sexiness of the medical clans' men."

"Hello there, ma'am. Are you alright? That was a close call you almost had with that wolf."

Luna almost fell in love with the man's voice. He had a charming flirting low tone to his voice. She could tell he wasn't from her world; he had an accent of one of the southern world's men. She realizes she was still staring at the man's body and immediately pulls herself together to speak.

"H, hi, um, thank you for saving me just now." Luna says nervously. "I hate those creatures. I was attacked by them before and barely got out with my life."

"You don't have to thank me. I was just passing by and happen to be in the right place at the right time."

"Well, I'm thanking you anyway. You didn't have to save me, but you did. Most people would have been too scared to interfere. Oh, and my name is Luna by the way."

"Luna, what a lovely name you have. You may call me Aaron. It is a pleasure to meet you. I must know, what's a beauty like yourself doing in these woods."

"I am on an important mission."

"I can't tell him to much information, I don't really know him like that so I will just skip the details."

"It must be a very important mission. I admire a brave strong woman like yourself. You are the first woman I've met to be out somewhere dangerous by herself."

Aaron walks over to her and caresses her soft cheek.

"Uh…thank you." she says nervously.

"Allow me to help you with the rest of your bags."

"This man is such a gentleman. I would love to be his wife. He is making me feel so warm inside. I know I must be careful who I choose since people are bond for life with whoever they sleep with. He would make an amazing first husband. Wait, what am I saying, I am sure he would not be okay with me having more than one husband. But there are so many hot and sweet men out there. How can I choose just one?"

After Aaron finishes putting the last bag on the wagon, he turns and smiles at Luna. "There all done."

"Thank you again. I guess I will be on my way then."

Luna was about to step into her wagon when Aaron suddenly walks in front of her. "Oh, you're leaving so soon. I thought maybe we could chat for a little while longer."

"No, I really need to get back to what I was doing. If you would like to chat more with me why not visit me when I return in a few weeks. Here, this is a map of my village."

"Interesting." Aaron says in his mind. "That's the village I was heading to. Now I know where my wife is staying. There is no way I'm letting this one get away. I must have her."

Aaron then grabs Luna by the arm and pulls her towards him. "I am not done with you."

Luna felt herself panicking. As she stares in Aarons eyes, she couldn't help but fall for him. She was starting to like the dominance he was having over her.

"Luna, do you mind if I make you my wife?"

"You want to bond with me? What's so special about me?"

"Not only are you beautiful but you are also brave to be out here alone. I feel a strong connection to you."

"I feel the same. They say bonds are strong and you never know when they will happen. I feel that you should be mines."

Aaron pulls her closer to kiss her passionately. He pushes her gently up against her wagon and holds her close.

"Mmm." Luna moans. "Your lips are so soft, and your grip is firm and strong, I love it."

Aaron begins to undress Luna and unbuttons his pants.

"Hah... hah... please don't stop." Luna whispers.

"I won't, I want to please you in every way?"

Aaron holds Luna's hands together and continues to slide down her panties and takes off his pants. He picks Luna up from the ground allowing her to wrap her legs around his waist. He slides his hard penis inside her. Luna lets out a loud pleasing moan as he begins to thrust and bounce her on his penis.

"Hah. Ah... Luna, you feel so good. I know you are enjoying this by how wet your pussy is becoming."

Luna holds Aaron even tighter as he pleases her. He starts kissing and licking her neck.

"Hah... Aaron you are so big I can hardly take it! I feel like I shouldn't be doing this, but you feel so good I don't want you to stop."

"I won't stop. I love the way you feel. You're going to be my wife."

Aaron walks over to Luna's wagon and lays her on her back. He spreads her legs wide as he kisses down her thighs. He began licking her pussy in a circular motion and sticking his tongue deep inside of her. Luna's legs began to shake. She grabs his head and pulls for him to go deeper.

He gently turns Luna around and slides his penis inside her. Luna can feel Aaron digging his nails into her ass as he pounds her from the back. Aaron smacks her ass and pulls her hair back. He flips her to her back and climbs on top of her. She wraps her arms and legs around him as he pushes his penis deep inside her once more. Luna screams his name over and over.

"Ah, Aaron you are so amazing. Faster, please faster."

Aaron begins to thrust faster as she begs. He bites his bottom lip as his eyes roll from the pure pleasure he was feeling. Feeling Luna's wetness was driving him crazy. They both fill the woods with their loud moans as they continue.

"I can't take this anymore! I'm going to cum so hard inside of you Luna."

"Yes! I want to feel you, Aaron! I'm ready to be your wife."

Aaron releases hard inside of Luna. They both let out a hard breath as they finished. A symbol of bonding love formed onto Luna and Aarons back.

"That was amazing Aaron." Luna says, still trying to catch her breath.

"It was, I loved every moment of this Luna. I knew I wanted you as my wife. I can tell you wanted me too. This is a moment I will never forget. But sadly, I must get going. I wish I could spend more time with my new wife, but I have important business to attend to, and you do as well. I know where you live, and we are bonded for life. I will always find you my dear."

He looks down at Luna and gives her a gentle kiss on the lips.

"Be safe on your journey my dear." Aaron says. "The exit of these woods isn't that far from here, so hurry."

"I will."

Luna hops in the front of her wagon to continue her journey. She thought deeply for a moment.

"If August was here would any of this have ever happened. I wouldn't have almost got attacked by a shadow wolf and I know August would have protected me. If only we didn't have that stupid fight, he might have been my husband on this journey. Then again, I wouldn't trade Aaron either. It's not like I wanted Aaron to stop making love to me. I felt something with him and wanted to bond with him. I want them both to be honest. Life just has other plans for me, I guess. I must stay focused on my mission right now. I have been everywhere so far. I believe I only have a few more villages to visit. When I am done, I'm going home to wait for my husband's return."

Luna laughs to herself. "Eve is going to kill me when I tell her this story."

CHAPTER 24

MESSAGE FOR A FRIEND

Weeks have passed since Eve heard from Luna. She hopes she was okay on her journey. At that moment of thought Meela came flying through the window with a message tied to her foot.

"Meela!" Eve slowly walks over to rub the fur on her cat owl's head. Meela let out a satisfying purr. Eve eagerly unrolls the letter; it was a message from Luna. She read that Luna had successfully given out Eve's message to unite the villages. Eve was overjoyed by how much Luna had accomplished. She will reward her for all the hard work she has done in the past few weeks.

Eve continues to read the rest of the letter. Luna had stated that her journey was long and exciting. She mentioned before she left the village, she and August had a bad argument and hoped to make up with him, she told Eve that she even managed to find a husband. Eve was surprised at Luna's next statement. She was happy Luna found someone. The next statement in the letter surprised Eve the most.

"Luna is what!" Before Eve could say another word, Meela let out a loud meow.

"Oh right! Could you deliver this letter to my mother Meela?"

She gives Meela a kiss on the head. "You are such a good girl." Eve says in a babying voice.

Meela gives her a meow purr as she takes flight out the window. Eve was thinking about what Luna said in her letter about the fight she and August had. She didn't know August was so upset. She never known August to act this way toward her and Luna.

"I must talk to August and see what's really going on with him. Meela is gone, how am I going to deliver this letter to him?"

Before Eve could think of an answer. Ronzell comes bursting through the doors. Eve just unexpectedly got her answer.

"Queeny! What are you doing out of bed! You are supposed to be resting. You are so close to giving birth."

Eve let out a laugh. "Ronzell, even I must stretch sometimes. I can't just lay in bed for months and not doing anything."

"Well, I guess you're right. I need to make sure that you are safe while you go through this pregnancy."

"I thank you for that Ronzell. Right now, I need to ask for a favor. I know you have high speed and you're great at stealth. You're also trained in fighting so I know you will be safe with the task I'm about to give you."

"Yes, I am all those things." Ronzell says raising an eyebrow at Eve. "So, what is it you need me to do honey?"

"I need you to deliver this letter to my friend August back in my old village. He's like a brother to me and I haven't heard from him in a while."

Ronzell looks at Eve and squints his eyes at her. "Is that it? I thought you were going to send me on some dangerous mission. not be a delivery boy."

"Please, Ronzell you are the only one I trust with this task." Eve says with a pouty face.

Ronzell let out a hard sigh. "Fine, give me the letter."

"You're the best friend a Queen could ask for."

"And don't you forget it." Ronzell opens the letter and reads it.

"Ronzell!"

"Don't mind me Queeny, I'm just making sure another man is not trying to steal you from the King."

"Never!" she says folding her arms. "I have never been more in love and bonded to Max. He means the world to me. No other man can even compare to him. I will never hurt the father of my unborn children."

"Calm down Queeny. I was just messing with you. I know your love and loyalty is to your husband. It's this August guy I don't trust."

"He's like a little brother to me. No need to worry. Plus, thinking of Max just makes my heart flutter. I can't help my actions around him. He always knows how to make me smile. And he drives me crazy with love."

"I know he does." He says giving Eve a little elbow bump.

They both let out a laugh and hugged one another. Eve really appreciated Ronzell. She watches as he readies his steed and sets off into the darkest of the night.

"Be safe Ronzell."

CHAPTER 25

HIRE OF THE ASSASSIN

Back in the village August paces the floor back in forth. "He should be here by now." August says frustratingly.

"Is it me your speaking of?" A man says from a dark corner.

August jumps back and grabs hold of his sword. He points it in the dark corner where the man is standing. "Who are you and how did you get in my house?!"

"It would be wise if you lower your tone." The man says. "You wouldn't want to cause a scene, do you? It may end with your death."

"I asked who you are?" August says nervously.

"You are August, right? You did send for me, correct?"

"You are the assassin I sent for."

The assassin let out a sigh of annoyance. "Yes, I am." The assassin says with irritation. "It seems you're not the smartest man I've worked with. Now if you don't mind, I would like to know what my job is that you want me to do. Who's the target?"

August slowly lowers his weapon but still holds it in his hand. He didn't fully trust the man he was about to hire. "The Dragon King and his head guard."

"Oh, two targets huh. That will cost you double. Are you sure you can afford it?"

"I figured it would be expensive. Here, this is most of my savings. I am sure it would be more than enough to get the job done."

The assassin walks up to a grey wooden box and looks inside. It was filled to the rim with gold and silver coins stacked in rows of twelve.

"This should be enough. So, tell me, why the Dragon King and his guardsman? Are they tyrants or something?"

"Yes. They also came and took someone very important to me."

The Assassin let out another sigh of annoyance. "This, important person." The assassin says quoting his fingers. "Wouldn't happen to be a Royal, would it?"

"Why does that matter?"

"You really are a fool, aren't you? You are aware of what happens if you kill a Queen's King don't you?"

"I don't want to hear your lectures! Can you do the job or not?!"

The assassin walks over and stands in front of August. "Who do you think you are talking to?"

August begins to tremble nervously. "S-Sorry I didn't mean it. I just been stressed okay."

"You should learn to control that tone of yours." The assassin says grinding his teeth. "You never know who you may come across that won't tolerate it."

"Your right." August says softly.

August and the Assassin didn't realize that outside the window, Ronzell had heard the whole conversation.

"I can't allow them to hurt my King and Queen." Ronzell whispers. "I must act now before everyone pays the price for Eve's idiot friend."

Ronzell bursts through the window and kicks August in the side. He was aiming for the assassin, but he dodged right before the attack.

"Who are you!?" The assassin asks.

"Someone who's about to kick your ass."

"He's one of the Queens men." The assassin says in his mind. "I must be careful they are known to be great fighters."

Ronzell jumps forward and clashes blades with the assassin. They struggle for a bit until Ronzell kicks the assassin in the stomach. The assassin flies backwards into the table. He lunges and attacks Ronzell. Ronzell blocks to shield himself from the attack. The assassin then fakes the attack. He spins and slices Ronzell in the side. Ronzell let out a scream as the wound was severely deep.

"You are finished!"

The assassin tries to strike Ronzell to finish him off. Ronzell quickly throws his cloak in front of the Assassin and disappears out the window.

"Who was that!?" He walks over to August and picks him up by the collar. "Did you try and set me up! Do you work for them?!"

"No! I have no idea who that person was I swear! And I'm not working for anyone."

"If I find out, you are working for the King or the Assassins clan I will have your head, do I make myself clear." He drops August on the floor and takes the money box. He then flees into the darkness.

August was on the floor in disbelief. "Was I wrong to hire a monster like him? He's gone now. I should have thought about this more."

August didn't realize that the assassin was still in the village. He creeps around the town looking for a certain house.

"There it is."

He limps to the door and knocks on it. Luna came to see who was knocking at her door so late at night.

"Aaron, you've finally made it back to me!"

CHAPTER 26

NO TIME TO EXPLAIN

Luna jumps into his arms and kisses Aaron passionately. She was about to speak when she notices Aarons clothes were torn and he held his arm in pain.

"Aaron what happened to you? You look like you've been in a fight or something."

"I was attacked by an unknown man in the village. Don't you worry about that though; he shouldn't be coming back any time soon."

"Well, thank goodness you are safe. There are many new people in this village now. We should be careful."

Aaron wanted to say something back, but he was distracted by Luna's belly.

"Oh, yeah this. Surprising right?"

Aaron places his hand on her round belly and smiles. "You're pregnant. I never would have imagined this."

Aaron leans in and kisses Luna.

"Luna this is exciting news for me. Unfortunately, we cannot raise our family here on this world. I need you to start packing immediately."

"Why must we leave? My friend is the Queen of this world, and she is really kind. I'm sure you will love it here."

"Wait, what did you just say?" Aaron asks with concern. "You are friends with the Queen of this world?"

"Yes. We grew up together. We are more like sisters. That night we met she sent me on a mission to save the people."

"So that's what you were doing in the woods that day."

Aaron paces the floor thinking to himself. "I can't tell my pregnant wife that I'm hired to kill her friend's husband. She will be devastated. She may die of shock with the news that I am an assassin in the first place. What a mess. What am I supposed to do? I should at least scout the Palace and see if that August guy was telling the truth. I don't want another mistake to occur."

"Aaron what is going on?" Luna asks with worry in her tone. "What are you not telling me? You can trust me you know."

"Now is not the right time Luna. I can't explain but you and my child are very important to me. So please, just trust me. I need you to pack your things okay."

Aaron walks to her and gently grabs her face. He stares deep into her eyes. She can see he is seriously worried.

"Okay I will pack my things. I assume you will be leaving again."

"Yes. I won't be gone for months this time. Be ready for when I return ok. I love you." Aaron kisses Luna and her belly and leaves out the door.

Moments later Luna hears another knock at the door. "Who could it be this time? Did Aaron forget something?"

Luna opens the door to see August standing there. "August! It's been months since we have spoken to each other. What are you doing here?"

"I needed to talk to you. I don't have anyone else to turn too."

August looks down to see Luna's round belly. "Luna. I wasn't aware that you were pregnant. Did this happen on your journey?"

"It did. If my stupid friend had gone with me, maybe this would have been."

"Been what Luna?" August asks softly. "Would have been my baby instead of whoever got you pregnant?"

"I don't regret the man I'm pregnant by. It's just, you were supposed to be with me okay."

August, reading her vibes, knew what Luna was trying to say. He walks over to her and gently grabs her chin and plants a kiss on her lips.

"August? Why would you do that now?"

"I may not be able to do that again that's why. I don't want to have any regrets."

"What do you mean?"

"I have done something awful Luna. I don't have time to explain but I was thinking in my home. I realize I must fix my mistake. I haven't been thinking of you or Eve's feelings and now something bad is about to happen because of me."

"August please, tell me."

"I'm sorry Luna, I am not about to drag you into this problem. Farewell, I must leave now."

August hurries and runs to his house to mount his shadow horse. He doesn't look back as he rushes out of the village.

"I must fix this. I can't allow that man to hurt them. I must warn them and turn myself in."

August left Luna standing in her home with a blank look on her face.

"What is going on? First Aaron, now August. Why do I have to pack? August sounds as if someone is about to be. No!"

Luna was putting the stories together. She was hoping that Aaron wasn't who she thinks he is. She also didn't want to think August had something to do with anything of the matter.

"I hope nothing bad happens to Eve. No! Eve is strong. I also heard rumors that her husband is one of the strongest Dragon Kings to be born besides the first King. I know they will be fine. It's Aaron and August that I am more worried about. Please, both of you, don't do anything stupid."

CHAPTER 27

<u>THE WARNING</u>

Back in the castle Eve hears a loud commotion outside of her door.

"Guards! Guards! Someone please, call for the doctor!"

Eve hurries and swings open the door. She screams when she sees Ronzell lying motionless in his own blood. "Ronzell!"

Max, hearing Eve's scream, came flying down the hall as fast as he could to her. He spots Ronzell on the floor and rushes to him. "Oh my gosh, someone call the doctor immediately!"

"Ronzell." Max says softly. "Who did this to you?"

Ronzell coughs as he tries to speak. "A...Assassin."

Max frowns at the news. "Ronzell. Where was he?"

"Eve's F... friend, August, house."

Ronzell struggles to give Max the letter that was supposed to be delivered. Eve looks shocked and hurt at the same time. She could never imagine that August would do such a thing. At that moment Dr. Lotus came rushing down the hall. He kneels and immediately starts to heal Ronzell.

Max looks over the letter and stares back at Eve. "Your friend is a traitor Eve." Max says trying to hold back his anger. "He hired the assassin to kill me."

Tears were falling from Eve's face. Max embraces her. He wanted her to know he wasn't' angry with her.

"Why would August do this?" Eve says with pain in her tone.

"Eve my love, you shouldn't stress yourself." Max says in a gentler tone. "You'll hurt yourself and our children. We will handle this situation."

Eve stares at Max. "I don't know what I would have done if I lost you. I don't think I would have lived long soon after."

"Eve! Do not speak like that. We are together now and will find our way through this together." Max grabs Eve's face and kisses her with great passion.

"I will never let anything happen to you or to myself Eve. So please let me handle August."

"What will happen to him? He's like a little brother to me."

"The sad truth is, he must be sent to the prism prison, and then sentenced to death. He betrayed the Palace and the people of this world. There is nothing we can do about the rules."

"This can't be happening. Why would August do this?"

"Well, one reason could be that he is in love with you. The other is that he is acting like an overprotective stupid brother. You said he was like family. Sometimes family do things that they think are best for others. You are a woman who can handle and make her own decisions. He doesn't even realize what he could have done. We are aware, thanks to Ronzell, that the assassin is coming. I will be on my guard."

Eve cries into Max's chest. "I don't care about any of the reasons. All I know is that I want to live a happy life with you Max. I will only love you."

"I know how you feel about me Eve. Now more than ever I will be closely watching you and my unborn children. There will be more guards watching you as well. I've waited a long time to get my hands on the assassin and I will be prepared for his arrival."

At that moment, Dr. Lotus walks over to Eve and Max. "Ronzell is stabilized. A moment later he would have been dead. I was able to close the wound and stop the bleeding. He will need to rest to regain his strength. Other than that, he's going to be just fine my Queen."

"Thank goodness." Eve says with relief. "Thank you for everything doctor."

"My Queen. This has been a stressful situation for you. As your doctor, I do advise you to go rest please. This commotion is not healthy for you and the children. I promise you; Ronzell is safe in my care."

"You're right doctor. I do feel weak and should lay down."

Max escorts Eve back to her room. He lays her down on the bed and strokes her flowing hair.

"This is all my fault Max. If I hadn't asks Ronzell to deliver that letter, he wouldn't have almost died."

"Think of it this way my love. If you hadn't asked Ronzell to do that, we wouldn't have known about the assassin trying to attack. Ronzell risked his life to bring that information back to us. I am thankful to have him here as your maid."

Eve smiles slightly. "Yeah, me too. I still can't believe August could be so stupid."

Eve starts to feel a hard squeezing pain in her stomach as she thinks of August again.

"Eve are you alright!"

"I'm fine Max. It's just the babies telling me to relax is all."

Max and Eve begin rubbing her belly.

Eve stares down at her belly and smiles. "Sorry for stressing little ones. I will try and relax, okay."

Max smiles as Eve talks to the babies. He could see how exhausted she was. She starts to close her eyes slowly as she falls asleep. Max watches her thinking about how he would prepare for the assassin's arrival.

A soft knock at the door takes him out of his intense thinking. It was Garret, he gestured for Max to talk with him. They whisper at the door trying not to wake Eve.

"I need you to scout the area, Garret. Also, find August and bring him to me."

"Yes, my King. I was thinking the same. Is the Queen alright?"

"She is, have your best guards always watching her."

"I will do as you ask, my King."

CHAPTER 28

THE INTERROGATION

Garret and his men set out to retrieve August. They were on the lookout for the Assassin who may be closer than they believed him to be. The night had started to rain and thunder as they made their way down the path. Garret spots a man riding towards the castle in a hurry.

"Everyone be on guard! This may be the assassin so stay sharp!"

"Yes Sir!"

As the man approaches, Garret recognized it was August. "August! Halt right there! You are under arrest for plotting against the King!"

"Please." Augusts begs. "I came on my own to explain and give warning."

"Save it. The King will be waiting to see you. Men take him to the interrogation room."

The men shove August to the ground and arrests him. They placed chains on his wrist and threw him in the back of their wagon. They traveled far and placed August in a dark cell. Augusts was frightened as he sat tied to an iron chair in a dark cold room. He could barely see the other guards present in the room. He knew this was a place of torture and misfortune.

"So, this is August?" Max says from the dark shadows.

Immediately August heart began to beat faster as he hears Max's strong voice echoing through the room. He can feel the pressure from the Kings aura filling the room. August has never sensed power like this before. The heavy weight of the King's presence feels like it was crushing August.

"My King this is supposed to be the Queens friend. He says he was trying to tell us why he hired the assassin."

"Is that so Garret." Max slowly walks around August, observing and studying him. He can see August trembling in fear. The guard pulls up a throne-like chair for Max to sit in. Max sits in his chair and leans his face against his fist. He stares at August from the shadows with his eyes glowing brightly.

"So, August." Max says in a calm authority tone. "What do you have to say for yourself? I am very disappointed that my wife's friend would try to cause harm to her husband. Not only that, but you also knew it would cause Eve and the people of this world to perish. Eve loves me and the people, I thought you would understand her knowing that you grew up with her."

"I…I did. I was angry. I thought I was slowly losing all the people I care about. I acted stupid and hired someone who I thought could help me. I really am sorry, so I came to warn you about my actions. I am prepared for the consequences."

"You actually think that your apology is enough!" Garret shouts angrily. "You were about to kill everyone because of your own selfish reasons! Only death awaits you!"

Max raises his hand for Garret to stop talking. "That is enough Garret." Max says calmly. "This situation is quite complicated."

"What do you mean my King?"

"He is still someone my wife sees as family. He doesn't even feel threatening to me. I can easily kill him now without even trying. Thinking about Eve is making this uneasy for me. I don't want to hurt her in any way."

"What would you have us do with him my King? We can't just let him go free after what he's done."

"No, we can't." Max let out a frustrating sigh. "Take him to the prison. I will be in my courters if you need me. I need time to think."

"You mean I'm not going to die!?"

"Garret could it be that Eve's friend is and idiot?"

"I don't doubt it for a second my King."

"One last thing before I take my leave." Max leans in close towards August. "I must ask. Are you in love with my wife?"

"N-No." August replies. "I will admit I found her to be attractive but there is someone that I fell in love with."

"Good." Max says with a grin showing off his fangs. "I would have killed you on the spot if you felt any other way."

CHAPTER 29

THE ATTACK

It had been a few weeks since the guards arrested August. Eve was in her room thinking about how she wanted to talk to August. She didn't know how to feel about the whole situation. Eve didn't know if she would have the right words to say to him. All she thought about was how she would punch him dead in the face for acting stupid. He was going to harm someone she truly loved, and Ronzell almost died because of his actions.

Still, knowing that Augusts was family, she hopes that he is learning his lesson from his actions. Knowing that he still lives means that Max has considered her feelings. She couldn't imagine what would have happened to August if Max had gone with his true feelings. The stress was getting to her. She knew she needed someone to talk to so that her mind could be at ease. Visiting her friend Ronzell was the only thing she thought about.

Eve makes her way down the hall to where Ronzell was recovering. Before she could even open the door, she heard shouting coming from the room. Eve opens the door to see Ronzell giving orders left and right to his maids.

"No, Place that there! You, go fetch me some more warm blankets! If I wasn't on bedrest right now!"

Eve laughs at Ronzell from the door. His maids are getting the full force of his authority. She guesses maybe they were used to it since they do work for him. Ronzell looks over to the door and sees Eve standing there.

"Queeny! You came to visit me. Ohhh, look at that belly! You are about to pop any moment. I must get well so I can be there for you."

Eve walks over to give Ronzell a hug. "I've so missed your presence, Ronzell. I see you got your spunk back."

"Oh, girl please. It will take more than this little scratch to put me down." Ronzell says as he gives Eve a little wink.

Eve looks down at Ronzell's wound. She could see it was more than a little scratch. This was a wound that was about to take Ronzell's life had it not been for Dr. Lotus's healing.

"Ronzell, I hate to bring this up, but can you tell me what the assassin looks like? It's been on my mind for a while now."

"Well, everything was happening so fast so I will try my best. I can remember he had slick dark blue hair that was combed back, the sides were shaved low. His chin was strong and slim. I remember him being a little shorter than I am. He had fierce looking eyes and wore a brim hat and trench coat."

Eve began thinking hard about the description. She felt like she heard of someone who looked like that before.

"Luna's husband!" Eve says quietly to herself.

"Um, Queeny. Are you alright?"

"I don't have time to explain. I must hurry to Max. I will fill you in later."

Eve gives Ronzell a peck on the forehead and rushes out the door. She hurries as fast as her pregnant body would allow her too. As she was walking down the castle halls she was spotted by Garret.

"Is everything alright my Queen?"

"No!" Eve says. "I need you to come with me to see Max."

"I shall accompany you, my Queen."

Eve swings open the door in a hurry. "Max, we need to..."

Eve was about to explain when she saw someone hiding in the shadows. "Max, look out!"

Max steps backwards spotting the assassin hidden behind the curtain. He kicks the assassin with great force against the wall. The wall cracks behind him leaving him vulnerable. He coughs as he tries to catch his breath from the kick.

Max could clearly see the man's face since his hat had fallen off.

"You!" Max says aggressively. "You are the one who murdered my mother and cause death to my father!"

Max had extended his claws and prepares to kill the assassin. "This is the end of your rampage!"

"Aaron don't do this!" Eve shouted. "You can't win a fight with my husband! I know you are Luna's husband. You should think about her and your child."

Aaron was shocked at what Eve had said. He remembered that Luna said the Queen was her friend. Aaron lowers his guard distracted by Eve. Before he knew it, Max dashes forward towards him with his claws extended. He stabs Aaron in his left shoulder. Aaron barely dodges the speed of Max who was aiming for his throat. His claws penetrated straight through the other side of Aaron's shoulder. He let out a cry of agony when Max pulls them out.

"You shall die today assassin!"

Aaron rolls and dashes for the window. Max grabs a hold of his cloak trying to yank him back. Aaron releases his arms from his cloak and jumps through the window.

"Are you okay my King?!" Garret asks.

Max ignores his question and manifests his flaming dark wings. "I'm going after him!"

Before Max could fly out the window, he heard a loud scream behind him.

"Max don't leave! My water... my water just broke! The babies, there coming!"

CHAPTER 30

BIRTH OF THE TWINS

Max looks over at Eve and rushes to her. "Damn it!"

"My King, I will send my men to search for the assassin. He couldn't have gone far with that wound. You go take the Queen to Dr. Lotus."

"Find him Garret! I want him dead or alive!"

"Yes, my King."

Max picks up Eve and flies towards Dr. Lotus's area.

"Max. I'm sorry. I had to go into labor at the worst time."

Max smiles at Eve, "No need to apologize my love. This is supposed to be a great time for us. We finally get to meet our babies."

Max rushes through the Palace when he finally arrives at Dr. Lotus's office. He opens the door and signals for Dr. Lotus's help.

"Oh my, looks like the time has come for your little ones to be born. Come follow me to the birth center. Lay her on the bed and help her into her gown please."

Dr. Lotus tells his assistants to prepare the room and bring warm water and towels. He couldn't help but notice the blood on Max's claws. Max communicates with Dr. Lotus without saying a word. Dr. Lotus gives him a clean bucket of water and a towel to clean himself. Eve let out a loud scream of pain.

"Max! Get your ass over here and hold my hand!"

Max's eyes widen. He hesitates for a moment as he was a little scared of his raging wife. He had never known Eve to raise her voice or be so terrifying.

"I said, get over here!"

Max hurries and gives Eve his hand. "What in the world is this grip you have? How are you this strong? I can barely hold your hand. Eve, maybe you should calm down."

Eve's eyes begin to glow brightly. She gave him a look that made him tremble.

"Don't you dare tell me to calm down! Would you like to feel what I'm going through!? You have no idea what I'm feeling! Where is Ronzell!? I want Ronzell here now!"

Dr. Lotus couldn't help but laugh. He put his hand on Max's shoulder and whispers to him.

"My King, never tell a woman giving birth to calm down. Leave that to the professionals okay."

"Yeah, I know that now."

At that moment, Ronzell comes bursting through the doors. "What is going on in here! Are you all treating my Queen with care? I knew something funny was going on around here. I don't have time for bedrest when Queeny needs me. Now, time to get to work. Where are the warm blankets and warm water! Where are the assistants? Do any of you even know what you are doing?"

Ronzell barks orders at all the maids and assistants in the room. They begin moving at a speed that they didn't have before. Ronzell rushes over to Eve and starts caressing her hair.

"There, there." Ronzell says in a babying tone. "Ronzell is here now love. Just calm down and breathe."

"Wait so he can tell her to calm down and not me?"

"Like I said before my King, leave it to the professionals. Believe it or not, it's different when the midwife or doctor says it."

"Max! Your hand now!" Eve shouted across the room.

Dr. Lotus tries to hold back his laugh as he can see Max's terror in his face.

"Go on ahead my King." Dr. Lotus says as he chuckles. "I will heal your hand when we are finished."

Dr. Lotus walks over to Eve and sits at the base of her. "My Queen, I need you to control your breathing and start to push for me. The babies are ready."

Eve relaxes and starts to push. She let out a cry of relief as her first child was born.

"It's a boy my King!"

The baby boy had small horns and glowing purple eyes. His hair was dark like his father's hair. It was long and flowed down his body.

"He's a Royal!" Max shouts with excitement.

Dr. Lotus lays the baby on Eve's chest as he prepares to deliver the next child. Eve gently kisses her baby's head. "He's so beautiful."

"Yes, he is my love."

"What will we name him Max?"

"Well, he is my first born. If it is alright with you, my love, I would like to name him after myself. Maximillian Dracon the 4th."

"I love it. I'm glad he gets to carry on your name."

"My Queen, it is time to deliver you your next child." Dr. Lotus says.

Ronzell takes a hold of her baby boy as she prepares to push again. Eve controls her breathing and begins to push.

"Oh my, this has never happened before. This is the first in history this has happened."

Eve was concerned. "Doctor, is something the matter?"

"Well congratulations my Queen. It's a girl."

Max was confused. "Doctor that's great news, but it's not rare for a Queen or common to have twins where one is a boy and the other a girl."

"That may be true my King. But there has never been record of two Royal twins and one is a girl and the other a boy."

"She's a Royal too!" Eve says with surprise. "I have never heard of anyone having two Royals at one time."

Dr. Lotus lays Eve and Max's daughter on her chest.

"She is so gorgeous Max."

"She has your beauty my love."

Eve's daughter had long flowing hair and glowing purple eyes. She was a mix of both her mother and her father's features.

Dr. Lotus couldn't help being amazed by such an event. "I will spread the word of this historical day my Queen. The people and Kings and Queens will talk about your family having this first miracle to occur."

Eve's excitement drops for a moment when she heard Dr. Lotus' words. He was going to spread the word of her birthing a Royal girl. She worries about her daughter and who she would be forced to Wedd in the future.

"Max. Will our daughter be forced to marry someone she barely knows?"

"My love let's not worry about that until the time comes." Max says gently. "Remember you didn't expect to love me in the beginning, now look at us. We are happy and in love, we have a new family now. Royals are born with a special bond and connection. It didn't turn out that bad for us because of that bond of love we share."

Eve gives Max a smile and pulls him towards her for a kiss. "You are right Max. I will be more open minded about the future of my daughter. It is her choice when all said and done."

"Let's just hope your family's line of hiding themselves don't fall on her." Max says jokingly.

Eve frowns at Max.

Max chuckles. "Uh, sorry my love. Was that joke to soon?"

Once again Eve couldn't find herself to actually be mad at Max. He is someone she loves and respects dearly.

"So, what would you like to name her since I named our son?"

"Silvia, Silvia Divine Dracon is her name."

"That is a lovely name for her my love."

"O-o-oh, can I hold her, Queeny?"

"Of course, Ronzell." Eve and Max both say.

Ronzell hands over Max Jr. to Max and picks up Silvia. He starts to baby talk as he cradles her. "Oh, my goodness, you are going to be my little baby model. Yes you are."

Eve and Max let out a laugh. They felt a little bad for their daughter. She is going to have so many outfits put on her and spoiled by Ronzell.

"Max, I know this isn't the right time to be talking about this but it's about Luna and her baby. I don't think she knows that the assassin, is well, the assassin. I trust Luna with my life and know she would never put me in harm's way."

"Why does this concern you, my love?"

"I feel like we should talk to her about him."

"Very well, I will arrange for us to go see her. For now, my men are out looking for the assassin. I'm sorry to say this but he is to be killed if spotted."

"No! She's bonded to him; she will die if you kill him!"

CHAPTER 31

THE SEARCH FOR THE ASSASSIN

Aaron was running as fast as he could through the woods. He felt the loss of blood catching up to him. He leans up against a tree and slides down to sit on the ground.

"This is the end for me. I will never see Luna or get a chance to meet my child. I will just have to let the guards end me here."

"Wow, I never thought I would hear those words come from your mouth." A man says from the shadowed trees.

Aaron was surprised. "Cortez! What are you doing here? Did the Assassin's clan send you to kill me?"

"Wait, what? No." Cortez says in a cheeky tone and chuckles. "I retired from the clan. When I heard they were still after you I quit so I may do my own thing."

Cortez walks over to Aaron and kneels beside him. He had on the same brown brim hat and brown trench coat as Aaron had on. His long flowing red hair was wrapped in a low ponytail. He was tall with gentle kind eyes. He wore an off-white shirt and tight dark brown pants. Being an assassin and tamer, he always carries a rope around his hip and two daggers. Just like Aaron, he had a red scarf tied around his neck. Cortez was known to be the only breed of his kind according to the people.

Aaron was still shocked by his response. "What do you mean you quit? You didn't have to leave because of me you know."

"Hey, you're the reason I joined in the first place. If they are after my bro, then they are after me as well. Now hold still so I can stop your bleeding."

Cortez was Aarons best friend. He was like a brother to Aaron. If he could trust anyone it was him. He always put up with Cortez's cocky attitude and overconfident ways. He would make jokes at the wrong time and cause trouble for Aaron. Aaron never cared about that. He was his family.

"So, did I hear right? You have a wife and a baby on the way? That's kind of fast didn't you just get here?"

"Yes, I fell for her in the Illusion Woods. She was about to get attacked by a shadow wolf."

"Oh, I get it." Cortez says in a sarcastic way. "Playing the hero, so she could give up the goods huh."

"What! Cortez, I would punch you if I had the strength."

"It's fine, I'm not judging." Cortez says giving a wink. "So, is she cute? If you are going to give up on life than I will have to step in and be her husband and father to the child."

Aaron looks angrily at Cortez. He then punches him in the arm.

"Ouch! I thought you didn't have any strength."

"I have just enough to kick your ass."

Cortez smiles at Aaron. "Good, then I don't want to hear another word about you giving up."

Aaron smiles back at his friend. He always appreciated the words he would give to him.

"If not, I will have to tag that wife of yours."

Aaron's smile turns into a sudden frown. He wanted to kill Cortez at that moment.

"So, can you walk bro?"

"Yeah, I can. Thanks for the help. But we must get out of here. The Royal Guards are after me."

"Yeah, about that. I have been following you and doing a little research of my own because I'm the best an all. You know that the King you went after is known to be the strongest ever born right? I also heard that the Queen is strong like the 1st Queen. I don't know how you even made it out alive."

"I knew it! I felt something strange about those two. Not only that, but they are also kind to their people. I'm going to have to kill that August guy for giving this impossible job."

"Nope. He has been captured by the guards. Seen it myself."

"Well at least I know he will get what's coming to him."

Aaron and Cortez hear a sudden massive growl coming from the shadows. Emerging from the darkness was the Alpha that attacked Eve before.

Cortez looks to the Alpha with Amazement. "Ohh, look. It's an Alpha shadow wolf and looks to be a hybrid."

"Cortez! We don't have time for your animal obsession!"

Cortez was very enthusiastic. "I'm going to tame it!"

"Wait!" Before Aaron could grab ahold of Cortez, he sees his friend leap in front of the Alpha.

"Hey buddy. Want some food?"

The Alpha growls at him and leaps to attack. Cortez jumps out of the way and threw his rope around the Alphas neck. He jumps on its back and starts beating the heck out of the wolfs snout.

"Tame! Tame! You will yield to me!"

Aaron rubs his temple as he watches his friend be absolutely ridiculous. The Alpha let out a screeching cry of pain as it fell to the ground. Cortez strokes its fur as he lays on it.

"Good boy." Cortez says in a low voice. "You didn't want me to kill you. You want to be my friend don't you?"

The Alpha gave his hand a lick showing approval of his dominance. Aaron looks on wondering how the heck Cortez keeps taming these beasts like that.

Aaron was annoyed. "Are you done Cortez? There are guards trying to kill me you know."

"Yep, I'm done he's my friend now."

"He must not be far from here!" A guard says in the distance.

"Cortez! We must get going! I need to get to my wife!"

"Well let's get to running."

As they were running through the woods Cortez suddenly stops and thinks.

"Why are we stopping! We are almost there!"

"Well, I just tamed the Alpha. We can send him to slow them down."

Aaron looks at Cortez with his eyes and mouth wide. "You want to send one Alpha wolf into an army of guards with swords and shields."

Cortez scratches his head. "Well, um. When you put it that way it sounds a bit silly right."

As they were speaking the guards caught up to them. "There he is!"

"Cortez."

"Yes Aaron."

"You're an idiot."

CHAPTER 32

ASSASSIN ENCOUNTER

Aaron and Cortez stand with their blades ready to fight off the guards.

"Aaron, you're still hurt. Just leave these guys to me."

Aaron sees that Cortez has taken on a more serious look. His friend may have been a goof ball but has never been bested in combat. Aaron and Cortez were the top two Assassins of the Assassin's clan.

One of the guards tries to rush them, before Aaron could blink his friend counters the attack slicing the man's arms off. He then dashes and slides behind the other guard slicing him down. Cortez throws a smoke screen and disappears into the mist. Aaron can hear the guards being defeated. More guards joined the scene but were confused in the mist. Cortez had hidden up in the trees and rain down kunai striking each of the men. One of the guards tries to retreat for help. He was quickly caught by Cortez and was stabbed in the back. Aaron gives a small clap of approval.

"Ah, I see you haven't lost your touch Cortez."

Cortez shrugs. "Yeah, it was nothing. Now let's get you to the village."

Back in the Palace Eve was still trying to convince Max to not kill the assassin.

"My love, please call off your men for now. I am telling you this so you can make the best judgement for when you finally capture him. I love Luna like a sister, and I don't want anything to happen to her. I already have to deal with August, and now this."

"Even if I do let them live you know I will have to kill your friend's son. He will surely try to seek revenge on me. That's how the story always goes. If they are all dead, then I have nothing to worry about."

Eve stares at Max for a moment. She tries to hold back the tears falling down her cheeks. Max couldn't stand the sight of the pain this was causing her. He let out a low growl.

(Sigh...) "Fine Eve, I will call off my men for now."

Eve lays her head on Max's chest and holds him for a moment. He holds her as he rubs her hair.

"Thank you, Max. I want this cycle of revenge and killing to end. I don't want anyone else to lose the people they love. When I am fully healed in a few days I would like to go see Luna."

"You will not go alone. Garret, the guards, and I will accompany you. If I find out that your friend is involved in this, then she must be punished as well."

"Very well."

Eve was confident that Luna was innocent. She didn't worry about Max's threat. All she knew was that the situation needed to be fixed soon before she loses both her friends.

CHAPTER 33

ESCAPE PLAN FAILED

A few days had passed, Aaron and Cortez had made their way safely through the woods.

"There is her house. Thanks for the help bro."

"No problem. Here, take these smoke bombs in case you need them. I will be heading home soon so get your wife and leave as soon as you can."

"I will."

Luna was at her home when she heard a noise in front of her door. She grabs her dagger and creeps quietly toward the door. She swung her dagger towards the opening. Aaron steps forward, catching her hand before she stabs him.

"Aaron! What is going on and where have you been? What happen to your arm!?"

"They are from my fight Luna." Aaron replies softly.

"Fight! Aaron there have been guards running all through this village looking for an assassin who tried to kill the King. You fit the description they described. Now tell me who are you?!"

Aaron let out a sigh. He didn't want to lie to Luna any longer. "I am an assassin Luna, from the Shadow Stalker clan."

Luna slaps Aaron in the face. "You didn't think I should have known about this. Not only that, but you also put the people and our baby's life in danger!"

"I'm sorry Luna. I never thought things would be like this. I wasn't expecting you and a new child. I had no idea you knew the Queen. Now I'm finding out I would have never been able to assassinate the King because of his strength. I was a fool and if I hadn't taken that job from that August guy this would have never happened."

"Wait, August hired you? I can't believe this, has everyone lost their minds or something."

"Look if it hadn't been for him, I wouldn't have met you." He says gently. "I don't regret anything but that I hurt you, Luna."

"Aaron." She says in a softer tone. "It says on this paper that you killed the King's mother."

"That was a misunderstanding. Plus, I didn't think anyone survived that world. I watched it crumble that day."

"Look Aaron we will have to leave this place. They will come after you."

Just as Aaron was about to reply they hear a hard knock on the door.

"Open up! This is the Royal Guards; we have the place surrounded!"

Luna shoves Aaron into the room and shuts the door. Luna walks up to the front door and opens it. She saw Eve, the King, and Garret standing at the front with the other guards.

"Eve!"

"Luna, we must talk to you about the father of your child."

One of the guards grabs hold of Luna's arm.

Eve frowns at his actions. "Hey what are you doing!?"

"We are taking her to the Palace my Queen."

Before the guard could make it out the door, Aaron comes rushing out the room and slices the guard's arm clean off. The guard screams in pain and passes out.

"She's not going anywhere!"

Garret pushes through the guards to reach Aaron. They pull out their weapons and begin to fight. They swing their weapons canceling out each other's blows. The battle went on until they knocked each other's weapons from their hands. Not stopping, the two men begin to throw punches. Garret swings and punches Aaron in the face. Aaron then returns a punch to Garret's face. They went on exchanging punches until Aaron was surrounded by guards. Aaron throws down one of the smoke bombs that Cortez had given him and flees out the window.

"He is running!" Garret shouts.

Max springs into action. "Not this time!"

Max begins morphing into his dragon form. Eve watches with her mouth wide as she had never seen such a massive Dragon before. He had shiny black and grey scales all over his body. His wings were those of the Great Griffon of Legend, beautiful and birdlike. His horns were extended up and back from his head. His fangs and teeth were large enough to rip any shadow creature apart with one bite. Max's body was as big as the Palace. He almost blows everyone off their feet as he takes flight.

"I have to hurry to the woods. I can at least make it out of here today then come back for Luna. I know her friend won't cause harm to her."

Max sees Aaron running and flies towards him.

Aaron looks back in shock at the oversize dragon flying his way. "Oh, no. I'm so dead if I don't make it."

Aaron runs even faster as he tries to make his way towards the Illusion Woods. He suddenly hears Max's thundering growl. Max's voice cracks and rumbles the lands and sky as he spoke. It was as if there was a devastating thunderstorm making its way through the skies.

"You are not going anywhere!" Max growls.

He blew out a large light blue flame from his mouth at Aaron. Aaron stops right before he was burned to death. The flames had covered the entire path of the woods. Max lands in a loud thud behind Aaron. The ground shook, knocking Aaron off his feet.

"You will die!"

"Max no!" Eve screams as she runs towards him.

"Eve, get away from here!"

"Max, listen to me! Killing Aaron will not bring your parents back. You are better than this! You are not a monster! You have been on this road for revenge your whole life, don't let this control your life!"

The guards were running with Eve. They finally catch up to Aaron. They forcefully knock him on the ground and arrest him.

"Max." Eve says in a gentle tone. "We have him. It's over now."

Max puts his head close to Eve. She begins to rub and comfort him.

"Please Max. Allow this man to at least see his child be born. Luna, she just went into labor."

CHAPTER 34

LUNA'S DESIRE

Luna was taken to a home right outside the castle to have her baby delivered. She sat in the room thinking about whether Aaron and her baby would be safe. She was prepared if Aaron was to be killed but she didn't want her baby to suffer because of the situation. Dr. Lotus walks through the room with a smile.

"Well, hello there." Dr. Lotus says in his calm low voice. "So, you are the assassin's wife. My name is Dr. Lotus. You don't have to be afraid of me. I will do no harm to such a beautiful woman as yourself."

Luna looks at the doctor up and down for a moment. "Oh, my, gosh." Luna says in her mind. "Eve was so right. He is definitely my type. So handsome and smooth talking. He even thinks my pregnant self is beautiful. Well, that may have been a lie since I am pregnant and in labor."

"Please relax. I will examine you for a moment. I want to check something out about the baby."

"Doctor." Luna says in a low voice. "I don't have anyone to talk to about this, but I really didn't know that Aaron was an assassin. I don't want anything to happen to me and my child."

Luna starts to tear up as she was explaining her story to Dr. Lotus. He gently rubs her cheek and smiles at her.

Dr. Lotus speaks softly to her. "You don't have to explain. I completely believe you. After examining your baby, you don't have anything to worry about."

Luna was puzzled by his words. "What do you mean?"

"You will know as soon as the baby is born."

"I don't understand you. You are so kind to me and calm about all of this. It's like you know something."

"Maybe I do. I am kind to you because you are innocent in all of this. Plus, I think you are beautiful, and a beautiful woman shouldn't be in tears."

Luna blushes at his words. "Doctor please don't tease me. I am pregnant and in labor, there is no way you think I'm beautiful. Also, how do you know I'm innocent. Please tell me doctor, I am so tired of everyone lying to me."

The doctor leans in and kisses Luna's forehead. Luna was surprised by his actions but didn't fight it.

He whispers in her ear. "I do find you attractive. I will tell you one thing, but you can't tell no other, okay."

Luna whispers back. "I promise."

"I know everything about the assassin or should I say Aaron. I know that everything will work out in your favor because of the kind heart the Queen has. She will never let anyone be hurt. She is a great Queen, and you are lucky to have her as a friend. But like I said, you must tell no one I know Aaron."

"I won't, promise. Thank you for those words doctor. I feel much better. You told me the truth, which I appreciate. Also, um, I find you attractive too, but I don't think it's the right time for me to be flirting you know."

Dr. Lotus chuckles. "I don't mind the flirting. Aaron will most likely be locked away, but he will be fine. I work at the prison as well so I will keep an eye on him. When that happens, I will have my chance with you my dear."

"Um, okay." Luna says shyly.

"I am such a sucker for men." Luna says in her mind. "Here I am flirting with the doctor when Aaron's life is on the line. Well, the Doctor did say that he might just be locked up. I wonder how he knows him and so much of the situation. Either way, I will find a way to get Aaron out of prison somehow."

Dr. Lotus looks over to see Luna staring at him. "Is there something you want to ask me Luna?"

"Well, yes. I would like to know more about you later. Right now, I don't even know your name."

"Miquel, Miquel Lotus is my name."

"What a hot name." Luna quickly covered her mouth as she realized she said that out loud. "Sorry about that."

Dr. Lotus let out a laugh. "It is fine. I found that to be funny. Maybe someday I will hear you call out my name."

Dr. Lotus gave Luna a little wink to gesture what he meant. Luna quickly nods her head yes at his meaning.

"I just feel so comfortable around you Doctor."

"It's been a while since I've had someone to talk to as well."

Luna and Dr. Lotus talked for a bit longer until Luna felt a hard pain in her stomach.

"Looks like it's time to deliver the baby Luna."

CHAPTER 35

THE DECISION

Eve, Max, and Garret were all standing outside the door waiting for Dr. Lotus to deliver the baby. Aaron was sitting cuffed next to Garret. The door opens, Dr. Lotus walks out the room with the baby in his arms.

"My King, My Queen, this baby is a boy. But you might want to have a look at him."

Eve and Max look at each other with confusion. They both rise from their chairs and walk over to have a look at the child.

"He's a Royal!"

They had a look of shock on their faces.

"Wait what! Please, may I see him."

Garret escorts Aaron over to see his baby. Aaron leans in to give his baby boy a kiss on the forehead.

"I shall give you my name since I know my life will end. I shall name you Aaron Shydon Jr."

Aaron looks up at Dr. Lotus. Dr. Lotus was giving him a look saying he better not say a word. He quickly catches on to his look and looks away. Aaron asks Eve if he may kiss his wife one last time. Max gestures to the guards to escort him to Luna.

Eve pulls Max over to the side to talk with him. "Max. Luna's son is a Royal born!"

"Yes, I see. This complicates things. If I kill the boy's father, he will grow up like me, seeking revenge. Maybe I should kill the whole family and be done with it."

Eve rolls her eyes at Max's words. He may be tough when it comes to his emotions, but he wasn't a cruel King. She had a better idea in mind.

"Or we can just raise the child in the Palace."

"What!"

"Think about it for a second Max. This boy is a Royal born and our daughter is a Royal born. Our daughter can at least have a chance to grow and get to know her future husband instead of being taken. I won't have to worry about the man my daughter marries because he will be raised by us. This is fate, and you know it."

"Augh! This is too much to think about right now. We will discuss this later. I need to go to a quiet place and think. Guards! Take the assassin to his cell. I will be heading back to the Palace."

Eve heads back to the Palace as well. She walks quietly into her room and spots Max sitting on the bed staring out at the stars. Eve sits behind him and wraps her arms around his chest.

"Max, what's wrong?" Eve asks in a gentle tone.

"The whole situation is what's wrong. The baby, his father, and your friends. I thought things would be simple. I was supposed to find my mother's killer and have him executed. My life has changed since I met you."

"Did I ruin your life, Max?"

"No." Max says in a softer tone.

He holds on firmly to her arms wrapped around him. "You are the best thing that has ever happened to me, and I love our new family."

Max paused before speaking again. "Eve, you said you want to see change in our world. So, what is it you are thinking? What will you have me do?"

Eve sits quietly for a moment trying to find the right words to say. She thought hard and was careful about the suggestions she wanted to give Max.

"Max. First let me say that I will never put everything on you. We are in this together. I will be with you every step of our journey. Let's start with August. I do believe he should pay for all the trouble he has caused. I see that you haven't killed him yet and I thank you for that. But if it wasn't for his stupid actions in the first place, we wouldn't have caught the assassin. I will let you decide how long he should be punished."

"Okay, that seems fair. He will stay locked away until I see that he has changed if that's what makes you happy. What about the rest of your suggestions?"

"Thank you, Max. Now, about Luna and her child. I wish for our daughter to grow up with the boy and get to know him. It would put me at ease knowing I can do that for Silvia. We wouldn't want her hiding her identity. One day she might feel the way me and my mother did in the past."

"No. We see firsthand the pain that causes people. As for the assassin, I will have him locked away forever. I know how much you love your

193

friend so that seems fair. We will explain to his son what his father has done to be in prison."

"That sounds like a great idea."

Max grips the sheets tightly. "This is still a stressful situation. I know we made our decision and I'm ok with that. But now, what am I supposed to do with all this build up anger?"

Eve gently kisses Max's back. He let out a small moan as he felt her gentle lips.

"I may have an idea Max. Use me to release your stress."

CHAPTER 36

STRESS RELIEF

Max stands and turns to Eve grabbing her by the throat. He leans down and kisses her passionately.

"I don't think you understand how much stress and anger I have built up, my love."

"Then show me my King. Let me feel all of what you are holding inside."

Max pulls her in kissing her aggressively. He throws her back onto the bed and rips the clothes off her body. He licks and sucks her body down to her hard nipples. He bites and nibbles on them while caressing Eve's pussy. Eve let out a loud moan as he pleases her.

"Yes Max! Don't hold back, give me more!"

Max rolls his tongue down to her already wet pussy licking deep inside her. Eve's legs start to shake. She always had a hard time handling Max's oral sex. He was more forceful with his tongue as he pleases her. She grips his hair firmly as her body trembles.

"Ah Max! Yes, keep giving me more!"

He starts to bite and lick her thighs as he rises from the floor. He pulls Eve into position and slides his hard penis into her mouth. Eve's back begins to arch as he strokes her throat faster. Max puts his hands around her neck feeling himself deep in her throat.

"Hah, hah, is this what you wanted Eve?"

Eve mumbles as she couldn't speak. He pulls out of her throat giving Eve a chance to breathe. Eve let out a hard breath. Turned on by his actions, she begins caressing herself as she stares at Max.

"Max that felt so good."

"Yes, it did, but I'm not done with you yet."

Max stands Eve on the floor and bends her over. He digs his claws in her ass as he pushes his penis inside her. "Ah Eve, your so wet."

Eve screams as Max starts pounding her from the back as hard as he could. Eve moans as she has an orgasm releasing her juices all over Max.

"Hah, I felt that. You're even wetter now."

He pulls her hair and spanks her ass as he continues.

Eve's eyes roll in her head as he pounds her. Max pushes deeper as he releases inside her. They both let out a satisfying moan as he finishes.

"Max, I want more. You are not the only one who has stress built up."

"Oh really, then show me your anger my love."

Eve pushes Max on the bed and mounts on top of his hard penis. They let out a moan as Eve starts to grind and kiss him. She places her hands on his chest and bends her knees to where her feet were planted on the bed. Max moans as she begins to bounce and ride him harder.

"Hah, Eve, I like what you are doing."

Max gives her ass a little smack as she continues to drive him crazy. He was enjoying the clapping of Eve's ass as it bounces on him.

"Eve! Keep going, I'm about to release so hard inside of you!"

Eve and Max were moaning so loud the guards could hear them outside the door. The guards stare at each other wondering what they should do. Garret looks at his guards gesturing for them to never speak about what they are hearing. The guards nodded uncomfortably of understanding.

Eve's nails were digging into Max's chest as she pleases him. "Your penis is getting harder! I can't take this anymore!"

Max holds her tight and thrusts up in Eve as she bounces. Both climax at the same time as they finish. Eve let out a moan as she fell over next to her husband. They both lay there catching their breath.

"So, did that help relieve some stress Max?"

Max takes on a satisfying grin. "Yes, I think that helped a great deal. We should be stressed more often."

Eve gives Max a little punch in the arm as they both laugh.

"Eve, you are really and amazing woman. I couldn't ask for a better wife and mother of my children."

"You are also an amazing man Max. I couldn't ask for a better man who cares about my feelings the way you do. You are and amazing husband and father."

Eve giggles. "You know, you changed my way of thinking. I was always running from my fate, my destiny. To be honest, I'm glad I did. I would have never met you and all the amazing people today. I wouldn't have met you the way I did. I love you, my King."

"I love you too, my Queen."

CHAPTER 37

<u>A NEW LIFE BEGINS</u>

Ten years have passed since everything happened. Eve and Max had three more children and were expecting another on the way. They have been raising Silvia and Aaron jr. together. Both are the best of friends now. Eve was always happy when she saw them grow together.

Often Luna would visit and spend time with her sons. She had given birth to two more Royals with Dr. Lotus. Eve would see the two of them sneak off into his private office. She knew they were probably making more babies. That wasn't a concern for Eve. She was glad to see her alive and safe.

Eve would see Ronzell as busy as ever. He was Eve's daughters' favorite person to hang out with. He would make them the cutest outfits and gave them whatever they wanted. Max was busy training their first son in small combat. He would teach him how to be kind and a good future King to be.

Leona, Eve's mother, would visit often. She would warp to their world and play with her grandchildren. Eve loved her siblings and even grew closer to her stepfather. He was kind to Eve and treated her as his own daughter. She can see why her mother loves him.

After Eve's mother leaves from her visit her father would show up to be with his grandchildren as well. He found a new wife of his own to love and continued to live a healthy life with.

As Eve walks the Palace grounds, she stops to look over to see Garret training her third child Melena. She was always fond of working out and running. Something Eve couldn't stand to do. Eve's daughter ran over to her and told her she would like to marry Garret when she is of age. Eve gives Garret a scowling look that made him nervous. She turns away and smiles to herself. She thought her daughter had great taste. Garret was a good man. Eve knew her daughter would be taken care of if he was her husband.

***

The next day Eve was strolling through the Palace to exercise her pregnant body.

A guardsman walks up to her. "My Queen, you have a guest out front."

Eve walks to the front of the Palace to see who was visiting. "Luna!"

"Hey there Eve!"

"Did you come to see Aaron jr.?"

"Yes and No. I came to pick up Aaron Jr. but also to speak with you. I come with news of me moving to a different platform."

"Wait, why? Is there something wrong?"

"There are too many memories for me here. I find it hard to stay here. Plus, I get lonely without you and August around. Not to mention my husband is in prison for life. Even if I do have a second husband, it's empty in the village without you two around. Dr. Lotus has been so busy lately, so it's best that I start a new chapter in my life. Don't worry I won't be far, and I will still visit you and Jr. I would still like to see my son marry that beautiful daughter of yours."

Eve and Luna lean in for a hug. "Luna I'm going to miss you. If you ever need me or in trouble you let me know, ok."

"I will. I will miss you as well."

"Mom? Mom!" Aaron Jr. shouts with excitement.

"Jr! There's my handsome man."

Aaron Jr. runs over and jumps in his mother's arms.

"Are you ready to see your father again?"

"I sure am!"

"Are the guards ready to escort us Eve?"

"Yes, they're ready."

Luna and Aaron jr. set off to the prism prison. When they arrived, they were presented with a large, massive shadow cube prison. The prison had a dark purple puzzle design on it that moved and lit up. It was heavily guarded with electric fences. The area they were in was always snowing. The blizzard snow made it hard to see what was in front of them sometimes.

Luna and Aaron Jr. step out of their carriage and enter the prison. They continue making their way through the prison when she suddenly spots August in one of the cells.

"August? Is that you?"

"Luna! It's been so long since I've seen you. What are you doing here?"

"I come to visit my son's father. I come often and never seen you in this cell."

"They moved me to this cell. I will be getting out soon."

August looks down at Luna's son. "Wow! He's a Royal born. Why would a Royal born's father be in prison?"

Well, do you remember the assassin you hired August?"

"Yes, I remember. I regret my actions every day because of it."

"Well, he is my son's father. He saved my life when I was on that journey Eve sent me on. He's not as bad as you think him to be, even though I didn't know he was an assassin."

"If I had been with you on that journey and not an idiot, I could have been the one to save you, or more. I wish I could still have a chance to be with you."

"Maybe you could. That's only if you accept that Aaron the assassin you hired as my first husband."

"You mean have multiple husbands? I wouldn't mind you know."

"Well, if you really are serious, then I will be staying on Eve's mother's platform. Find me whenever you are free. I will be living in the forest isolated from the people. I must go now. Hopefully, I will see you soon."

Luna left August thinking of her offer. He watches her as she walks down the hall. Luna walks farther down the prison to where they were keeping Aaron. As she reaches the door she trips and falls into the guard standing in front of his cell.

"Sorry, I'm pretty clumsy today." Luna says with an awkward laugh.

"It's alright. You may enter now."

There were always two guards guarding Aaron's cell. The one on the right opened the door. "Aaron, you have visitors."

"Aaron!"

"Luna!" Aaron stands to his feet and walks over to Luna.

"Junior, look at you! You are getting so much older. I missed you two so much."

"I missed you too father. I'm getting handsome just like you."

Aaron laughs and hugs them both. "Yes, you are son."

They sat and joked with each other for a while. Luna looks towards the door to make sure no one was listening. She leans closer to Aaron and whispers.

"Aaron. I'm going to be moving to Eve's mother's platform like we planned. I'm going to live in that location we talked about. I also have a plan for you if this works out."

Aaron whispers back. "What do you mean?"

"Times up!" The guard shouts.

Luna quickly pulls Aaron close and kisses him. She then slips the guard's key hidden under her tongue into Aaron's mouth. Aaron's eyes widen, he slips the key under his tongue.

Luna gives Aaron a little wink. Aaron smiles at her knowing what he must do next.

"Till we see each other again Aaron."

"Until then Luna."

ABOUT THE AUTHOR

Hey there readers. First, let me say thank you for taking the time to read my story. I really appreciate it. I have always loved writing and creating stories. I usually get inspired by other books similar to my own. My favorite books have always been fantasy, books about out of this world creatures, and mythical beings. I like to separate myself from real life, I never like to write anything about our world today. You may notice my love for hot steamy scenes. This is something that I look for in other books I enjoy but often can't find it. So, I thought, well why not write it myself and put all the naughty things that I enjoy in my books. I not only write books but also enjoy the love of gaming. I grew up as a gamer girl and I still play games to this day. I Love those RPG games, puzzles, shooters, adventures games. You name it, I've probably played it. My last, but not least, passion is drawing. I have been drawing ever since I was a kid. You may notice I draw my own book covers and make art daily. It's something I do to clear my mind, now I use it to bring my characters to life. I hope you all stick around to enjoy the rest of my series for THE E.N.D'S TALE and many more steamy love books to come. Again, thank you for all your support.